SINISTER ATTACHMENTS

A Paranormal, Psychological Thriller

Sometimes, resentful spirits pursue souls until they get what they want—vengeance and sinful pleasures.

(Book 1) After Maggie McGee's husband had committed suicide in their home, Maggie needed a place to live that would not remind her of the recent tragedy. She finds an affordable apartment in an old building sitting on a bluff along the shoreline of Lake Michigan. Maggie knew the building used to be a tuberculosis sanatorium, later transformed into a psychiatric hospital until finally closing its doors in 1969 due to patient abuse. However, what she did not know was that sometimes, sinister attachments from the past pursue souls until their evil needs are satisfied. Maggie questions her sanity and grasp of reality, as diabolic and envious predators work against her in this paranormal, psychological thriller.

ConnieMyres.com

SINISTER ATTACHMENTS

A Paranormal Psychological Thriller

by

CONNIE MYRES

Feather and Fermion Publishing - Michigan

CONNIE S. MYRES
FEATHER AND FERMION PUBLISHING
MICHIGAN, USA

CONNIEMYRES.COM

Dedicated to my family and friends, especially my sons Lucas and Charles Kraus for their loyal support and encouragement of all my projects. I appreciate you.

Turn back now, before it's too late.

ONE

MARGARET "MAGGIE" MCGEE drove her compact car into the parking lot of Sandpiper Bluff Apartments. She turned off the ignition and looked at the renovated apartment building. While not restored to its previous duties as a tuberculosis hospital, most of the decor from its earlier life as Lake Shore Sanatorium remained intact.

Situated atop a rare steep clay bluff, on the shore of Lake Michigan, the 1899 three-story brick building looked nothing like a hospital. Rather, it resembled a hotel for the elite. Open double-deck porches that once allowed sufferers of tuberculosis to breathe in the cool fresh air blowing off the Great Lake, still wrapped around the building. Shutterless tall windows added balance to the dormers protruding from the sloping roof covering the third floor. Two large old brick chimneys jutted out through the roof, showing testament to the coal-fired octopus furnace and wood stoves they used to serve.

Maggie knew of the old sanatorium but never saw it until she responded to a vacancy ad in the South Haven Record.

Energy-efficient, two-bedroom, furnished apartment with updated appliances. Enjoy privacy and peace in this historic and renovated building under new management and renamed to Sandpiper Bluff Apartments. Walk the sandy shores of Lake Michigan and relax with the view of beautiful sunsets seen from the apartment, perched high on a bluff. Affordable rent and flexible lease.

When she attended Bloomingdale School, she had known about the sanatorium being haunted. It had become a favorite tale every Halloween when students would set plans to visit the spooky abandoned building, hoping to catch sight of the paranormal.

They would begin the scary campfire story by telling how it used to be a hospital for the wealthy suffering from tuberculosis. Then in the 1950s, after the streptomycin antibiotic was discovered and tuberculosis was no longer a threat, the building's management brought in psychiatric patients to replace the lungers.

After rumors of staff abuse toward the mentally ill residents had been found to be true, the sanatorium closed down in 1969. It sat vacant for decades, until a real estate developer came in, restored the dilapidated grand building, and converted the already hotel-like rooms into apartments. But as the story goes, renters never stayed long. Many even broke their leases, claiming ghosts were driving them from the building. So once again, it sat with rooms nobody wanted to rent.

But Maggie thought it was perfect. Aside from the fact that she had never seen a ghost or anything paranormal, for that matter, she needed a place to live and the price was right. The low rent did cause her to wonder why an apartment on the shoreline was so cheap. Theowner could charge an arm and a leg or turn it into a secluded resort for celebrities. But no one had done that.

Maggie had found her husband, Cory McGee, dead in the dining room of their Breedsville home a month earlier. A handgun lay on the floor beside the chair he had been sitting in when he decided to take his life. Maggie had no clue he was in such a state of mind, they planned an addition to their home the week before.

Maggie popped the trunk and got out of the car. She walked to the back, took out her wheeled suitcase and backpack, and then walked toward the sidewalk. Her suitcase rumbled as it rolled over the concrete pavers leading to the porch steps. She stopped a moment and admired the old-fashioned roses climbing the columns of the whitewashed porch. Their aroma was better than any store-bought perfume.

The summer sun was high in the azure sky as she looked up toward the roofless second floor porch, sitting on the first. She had seen old pictures of the sanatorium; it was almost like stepping into the past. The property developer certainly knew what he was doing when he restored the old place.

Her second-story room faced the lake. She had only been in the room once, to inspect it and sign the lease. Before she even arrived that day, she knew she was taking it and moving in as soon as they would let her. Even if she saw a mouse run across the countertop, she was moving in. The magnificent view and tranquility would be worth setting a couple of mousetraps.

The breeze blowing off the lake was brisk. She could hear the waves crashing below the bluff and smell the fresh moist air. She took a deep breath, filling her lungs with the fragrance of roses and the scent of nearby pine and spruce trees.

Maggie smiled and continued walking toward the porch. She tugged the suitcase up the steps and stood in front of the large wooden double door. Before walking inside, she looked along the length of the porch. Wooden porch swings swayed gently on either side of her. Potted ferns hung from the ceiling, spaced at intervals above the porch rails. The place was more like a bed-and-breakfast than an apartment building. She was going to like it here.

She pushed open the door and walked into the vestibule. A dozen or so mailboxes were flush against the wall ahead, a chair sat to the left, and a buzzer panel was on the right wall next to the inside glass panel door. Each button on the panel had an apartment number beside it; she needed the supervisor, Mr. Carl Zimmerman. She found it and pressed the black button until it buzzed through the panel's speaker.

There was no answer. Thinking the door could be unlocked, she pulled the handle, but the door would not open. Someone would need to let her in.

She pressed the buzzer again. This time a gruff voice came through the speaker.

"Yes?" the man said.

"Mr. Zimmerman, this is Maggie McGee, I need in my room."

"Didn't I give you a key?" the superintendent asked. "No, I guess you forgot," she said.

"Meet me at my office and I'll get you one. I'll be right down," he said, buzzing her in.

A waft of fresh paint, mixed with old building smells, drifted into her nostrils as she opened the door. Her nose
wrinkled; she did not remember the damp wood odor the last time she was there.

Mr. Zimmerman's office was directly ahead, past a welcome desk. Years ago, it had to have been the reception desk for incoming patients and visitors, she thought.

While she waited for the apartment supervisor to come down the elevator, she looked around the lobby. Newer windows were placed inside the restored dark stained wooden windowsills. Gilded plaster molding joined the walls to the ceiling, and the oak wooden stair rails, leading to the upper floors, were polished to shiny perfection.

The door to the old elevator clanked open. Mr. Zimmerman walked out as though he had been awakened from a nap. The few strands of gray hair that were still on his head lay this way and that. His round belly smoothed the fabric of his white tank top. Likely from beer, Maggie thought.

"Hi, Mr. Zimmerman," Maggie said. She knew she appeared too cheerful, but she could not help herself. Aside from the fact, there was no way she could live in the house Cory had committed suicide in, she was excited to move into her new home. She had spent the last month living with her best friend Jessica Pinter in a rundown mobile home. Sure they were close, but Maggie felt that if she stayed there too long they would be at each other's throats. They were not arguing yet, but Maggie could tell it was only a matter of time.

"How are you doing?" Mr. Zimmerman asked as he walked past her, toward his office. An unlit Churchill cigar bounced in the corner of his mouth as he spoke. "Sorry, I forgot to give you the keys."

"Not a problem," she said, walking behind him.

Mr. Zimmerman unlocked the office door, walked in behind the desk, and lifted two keys from the wall hooks.

"This one is for the entrance," he said, handing her a key that looked like a standard house key. "This one is for your apartment, 22C." The second key, however, looked like an old-fashioned skeleton key. He looked at her suitcase. "Is there anything else you need help with?"

"No, I got it from here," she said, holding the keys, moist from his sweaty hands.

Mr. Zimmerman followed her to the elevator. He stepped inside behind her and pushed the second floor button. "My apartment is on the third floor if you happen to need anything." He paused and then said, "This building has been here over a century, so it does a lot of groaning and creaking in its old age."

Groaning and creaking. Sounds from the bones of the old hospital, not ghosts, or goblins, she assured herself. "Thanks, Mr. Zimmerman. If I need anything, I'll call you."

The ancient elevator door rattled open. The renovators certainly did not bother with replacing the elevator, only restoring it to working condition. Maggie stepped out, her suitcase clunked over the partition between the elevator and the floor.

"Good luck," Mr. Zimmerman said as the elevator door closed.

Good luck? What is that supposed to mean? She turned back to look at the superintendent, but the door had already closed.

To her left was the open stairway leading back down to the foyer and up to the third floor. A wooden railing encircled the open staircase was partially attached to the

northeast corner of the building. She could hear the elevator door open above and the heavy steps of Mr. Zimmerman walking down the hall to his room. Noise traveled easily through the building's interior.

Maggie stood in the hall a moment, looking at the layout of the second floor. Past the stairway and the elevator were two doors leading out to the second-level porch—one to the east and one to the west—leaving only enough room for three good-sized apartments. Apartment 20A occupied the southwest corner of the building, apartment 21B took up the southeast portion, and Maggie's apartment, 22C, sat in the northwest corner. She had not met any of her neighbors, but there would be time to get acquainted later.

Plenty of light spilled into the space through the delicate lace panels of the French doors leading outside. She had a hard time envisioning patients in wheelchairs and hospital beds being pushed through the doors and out onto the porch to breathe in the fresh air, the supposed cure for tuberculosis.

Maggie turned right and walked past the utility room that sat between her apartment and the elevator. Good thing that room was there or else she would hear the rumble of the elevator ascending and descending, she thought.

She walked up to her door, let go of the suitcase, and placed the antique key into the lock. It was awkward turning the lever lock, but after a couple tries, she was able to turn and unlock it. She opened the door, took the handle of the suitcase, and rolled it inside, closing the door behind her.

After sitting her luggage next to a full-length mirror and coat rack, she walked straight ahead through the

living room and looked out one of the windows. The view was awe-inspiring. With the building sitting so close to the bluff, and with the veranda blocking the view of the ground, it was as if she were on a ship looking out across a vast ocean.

She opened the window before going into the small galley-style kitchen. A tiny dinette table was pushed against the wall, next to a window. She looked at the rust-stained sink and along the empty countertop, she was happy not to see any mice running next to the backsplash. She opened the refrigerator; it was empty. "I knew a welcome basket of food would be expecting too much," she whispered, then closed the refrigerator door.

She walked out of the kitchen, toward the two small bedrooms. Each room had a north-facing window and view of the shoreline as it stretched toward Saugatuck.

Then her cell phone rang. It was Nora Bella, her literary agent.

"Hi, Maggie. Are you all settled into your new writing studio?"

Maggie gave a halfhearted laugh. "I just walked in the door."

"The publisher wants to know if you're going to have book four done soon," Nora said. "I know you've been through a lot, lately, but the show must go on."

Maggie shook her head, wishing she had let the call go to voicemail. "I'm working on it. I was just getting ready to pull out my laptop." Not.

"I have a call coming in," Nora said. "I'll call you in a couple of days."

The call reminded Maggie that she had told Mr. Zimmerman that she was an author. And how Nora was always bugging her about the progress of each book in

her series, Raven Ridge Mysteries, like a dog pestering its master to go outside and play. She had told him how Nora's favorite saying was, "Maggie, you know the deadline is soon . . . Chop, chop." And that she needed seclusion so that she could write and keep Nora happy. That had to be what he meant when he said, "Good luck."

TWO

MAGGIE YANKED OUT a shopping cart from the one in the row ahead of it and pushed it into the small grocery store. The only cashier in the store was busy checking someone out as she pushed the wobbly wheeled cart past her toward the produce department.

She placed potatoes, bananas, lettuce, and tomatoes into the metal-framed basket. Bread and condiments were next. Deli meat and salads were too tempting to pass up as were coffee and beer.

She took her time walking down each aisle before deciding this would be the store she would frequent, especially since it was so close to her apartment.

When she got up to the checkout, she asked the cashier about the store hours. The middle-aged woman, wearing a green apron with Lenny's Grocery written across the bib in big white letters, answered Maggie's question and then asked, "Are you new here?"

"I haven't lived too far from here; I'm just new to this area."

The cashier smiled as she continued to ring up Maggie's groceries. "You'll love it here. I've lived here all my life and never plan to move."

"It is a beautiful area," Maggie said, pulling the wallet from her purse.

"So where do you call home now?" The cashier asked as she rang the last item and pointed to her name badge. "And, by the way, my name is Valerie, people just call me Val."

"Nice to meet you, Val. I moved into the Sandpiper Bluff Apartments today, and I'm here picking up my first set of groceries," Maggie said, swiping her card in the payment terminal. She put the card away and looked at the cashier who was staring at her. Maggie smiled, but the cashier did not smile back. "Is something wrong?"

The cashier turned back to the register, took the receipt, and handed it to Maggie. "Do you know about that place?"

"What do you mean? Are you talking about ghosts? I know it used to be a sanatorium for people with TB, and later it housed the mentally ill." Maggie looked to her side as an elderly woman sat a cantaloupe and a can of prune juice on the conveyor belt.

A look of concern spread across the cashier's face. "That old sanatorium sets way back in there. It is so deep in the woods that you can't even see it from the road. But obviously, you are already aware of that. The wind blows in there hard, and when winter comes you get stranded, and the electricity can be out for days."

Maggie put the grocery bags into her cart. "Winter is a long way off. I'm sure they have someone who keeps the road to it plowed."

The cashier looked at the old woman, then back to Maggie. "Let me get to the point. You may think I'm crazy, but I don't think people have been there much lately, and when they are, they come up . . . missing. To tell you the truth, I didn't realize it had reopened for business."

Maggie stared at the cashier, this time. She felt a sense of dread wash over her. "Mr. Carl Zimmerman lives there."

"That old codger," the old woman behind her said with a loud whiny voice. "He's nothing but a stinkin' drunk. I'm surprised he's still alive. He used to charter fishing boats out of Lighthouse Marina." The wrinkled woman stopped talking long enough to cough and then continued. "My daddy once said Carl killed a man out there on the water, right there in front of Lake Shore Sanatorium—all liquored up on Scotch, he was."

Maggie could not believe what she was hearing, or seeing. An old lady's daddy was talking about Mr. Zimmerman? Had to be Mr. Zimmerman's father. The old woman did not know what she was talking about; she had to be senile.

"That place is cursed," the old woman blared as Maggie pushed her cart of groceries out the door. "Don't go back there or you'll regret it, girly."

THREE

MAGGIE FINISHED PUTTING away the food, opened a can of pop, and then placed the laptop from her backpack on the dinette table. She plugged it in and opened the top. This would be a good place to work, she thought as she looked out the kitchen window next to the table. A far-off sailboat floated in the haze of the distant horizon while a flock of seagulls flew down toward the beach. A little distracting, but she could handle it.

She took a sip from the cold can while replaying in her mind what the women at Lenny's Grocery had said to her. They thought no one was living here; she whispered as she watched the laptop wake up. No one here? Of course there was. Mr. Zimmerman was here, and there was a car in the parking lot.

Then she heard an apartment door open. She quickly got up and tiptoed to the door's peephole. She saw a woman with a headband and wearing a paisley print dress leave apartment 21B with a child at her side. There, proof she was not the only one in the building.

Having been unnerved by the women in the grocery store, she decided to prove them wrong and introduce

herself to her new neighbor. She opened the door and walked into the hallway. She smiled and said, "Hi."

The woman took the young girl's hand and stopped at the top of the stairway. She looked at Maggie, seeming a bit surprised due to the fact she did not say anything for a moment while she studied Maggie's face. "Hi, did you just move in?"

Maggie left her door open and walked toward the woman and child. "My name's Maggie. I just moved in today. This sure seems like a nice place."

"My name's Debbie and this is my daughter, Susie. It's nice to meet you," she said, extending her hand in greeting. "And yes, I agree, this is an excellent place to live."

"Have you been living here long?" Maggie asked, releasing her hand from Debbie's overly firm handshake.

"We've been here a long time. So has Bruce," Debbie said, pointing toward apartment 20A. "He's a cool head."

Cool head? Maggie was not sure what that meant; must be a throwback saying from the 1960s. She smiled and nodded. Then she said, "I know Mr. Zimmerman is on the third floor, is there anyone else in the building?" Maggie needed to know the place was full of life and not dead empty.

"Downstairs is Ethel. She calls herself a seer. I think she uses that crystal ball as a ruse, I wouldn't trust her. She keeps to herself; she's out of her tree," Debbie said, rolling her eyes. "Her apartment would be directly below yours. We don't talk to her much though."

Maggie felt better knowing she was not alone. She turned her attention to the girl standing next to Debbie. Her hair was long and scraggly; she wondered when it

had last been brushed. Maggie held out her hand. "It's nice to meet you too, Susie. How old are you?"

The girl looked up at Maggie through strands of dark hair, partially covering her face. She did not say anything. "She's ten, and she's a little shy," Debbie said. She cocked her head and asked, "So what do you do for a

living?"

"I'm an author," Maggie said. Even though she had been writing full time for a couple of years, it still felt strange to say it. Her old identity as a nurse was still hard to shake.

Debbie smiled a big, broad smile. "So, does that mean you're home most of the time?

You writers do spend your days typing away in seclusion, don't you?"

Maggie could tell Debbie had something on her mind by the questions she was asking. "Yeah, I suppose."

Debbie looked down at Susie, still holding her hand. "I work nights at the hospital and it is so hard finding someone who can watch Susie overnight. Would you mind helping out? My last babysitter just quit, and I need someone immediately," she looked at Maggie's bland expression. Maybe it was an expression of shock. "It would only be temporary . . . and I'll pay you, don't you worry about that."

Maggie was totally regretting having come out into the hallway to introduce herself. It was not that she did not want to help, but she did not even know this woman. If she said no, everyone at Sandpiper Bluff would probably shun her. If she said yes, then who knows how long Debbie would have her babysitting. Maybe Susie will sleep most of the night. She was not a toddler, but it would still put a damper on her writing and the

upcoming deadline for book four. "I can help a little while, but I do have a lot of work to do."

Debbie hugged Maggie. Her blue eyeshadow and dark eyeliner made her look like a Barbie doll. "You don't know how much this means to me. Bruce isn't good with kids, so I haven't asked him. Besides, Susie doesn't want him to babysit her. Someone like you, Maggie, can play with her and keep her company."

What am I getting myself into? Maggie was so angry with herself for accepting the babysitting job. She should have thought of a white lie, but her mind did not work that way. Too late now, she was stuck. Maggie smiled.

"I work Friday night; can you begin then?" Debbie asked, pressing her pale pink lips together in anticipation. Friday was two days away. Maggie had wanted to explore the area and meet her friend, Jessica, for a few drinks. Those plans would now have to be postponed. Besides, this Debbie did not even know Maggie; she could be a serial killer or child molester for all Debbie knew.

Maggie was never good at saying no. "Sure, that would be fine, but you don't even know me."

"You look like the trustworthy type," Debbie said, pulling little Susie toward the stairway. "I feel like I've known you forever."

Maggie stood there, shocked at what had just occurred. Crazy people surrounded the home of her dreams.

As Maggie turned to walk back toward her apartment, the door to apartment 20A opened; a man slightly older than she stood in the doorway. His dark hair was combed into a high mound over his forehead, similar to the pompadour haircut of Elvis Presley and James Dean. "Hi, I heard you and Debbie talking, and I just wanted to introduce myself; I'm Bruce," he said, opening his door wider. "Would you like to come in?"

Bruce was certainly pleasing to the eye, but she thought she had better get back inside her apartment before she committed to some other duty. "Hi, I'm Maggie, your new neighbor. And sorry, but I have lots of work I have to get started on . . . Deadlines and things."

He smiled. "Well if you need anything, anything at all, I'm just next door."

"Thank you, Bruce," Maggie said, watching him close the door.

She walked back inside her apartment and locked the door. The people here seemed friendly, but a little odd. A fortuneteller in the building? Why would I have expected anything less? she thought.

FOUR

THE DOOR BUZZER sounded like a bumblebee trapped inside the wall, jolting Maggie from the imaginary world of her story. She had been up early that Thursday morning, working to beat her book's deadline. She rubbed her eyes, quickly saved her document, and rushed to the intercom.

"Hey, Maggie, it's Jess, let me in."

Jessica Pinter has been Maggie's best friend since third grade. They know each other better than anyone else does, including their families. Maggie knows that Jess backed her car into the boss's parked vehicle, leaving a big dent in the front quarter panel of Mr. Hall's black Cadillac. She never reported it or told anyone, except Maggie. She told her how he ranted for a week about it and that he knew whoever did it had a white car because of the paint left on the crushed metal. Since the bumper of Jess's car had black paint on it, she was afraid to drive it to work anymore, fearing she would be fired if he found out she did it and never told him. So she started driving her brother's car, telling him hers was in the shop.

And Jess knows that Maggie faked being sick so that she would not have to spend her only week of summer vacation with her in-laws, in a secluded cabin in the woods. There would be nothing to do but play cards, watch squirrels climb trees and listen to his family gripe. They wanted Maggie to stop that ridiculous pie in the sky idea she had about making money writing while praising Cory's every move. It would have been pure torture.

"Maggie, dear," Mother McGee would say in her usual hoity-toity voice. "You know as well as I do that the odds of making any money from your writing are unrealistic. Who do you think you are? Agatha Christie?"

Talk about a kick in the gut. Yes, pure hell.

Maggie stood in her open doorway as Jess walked up the steps, twisting her head to look at the architecture of the old hospital.

"I'm over here," Maggie said, happy to see Jess.

Jess walked into Maggie's apartment holding a fruit basket and a bottle of wine. "Wow, I can't believe you're living here. This place is about as creepy as they come."

"Thanks for the nice housewarming, Jess," Maggie said, closing the door.

"The view is spectacular," Jess said, taking the basket and wine into the kitchen. "But I still don't think it's worth living here."

"I know, I know," Maggie said, uncorking the wine bottle. She then took her only two drinking glasses from the cupboard. "I haven't had a chance to go down to the beach, yet. Do you want to go?"

"Absolutely," she said, taking the wine bottle. "Have you met your neighbors yet?"

Maggie scrunched her nose. "Yeah, they're a little on the odd side. I even have to babysit tomorrow night, and I don't even know these people."

"I would've refused," Jess said. "I think that's asking a lot of someone who just moved in."

"The guy in apartment 20A is kind of cute, though," Maggie said, walking toward the door. Then she stopped and brought her hands to her face as tears filled her eyes. A surge of mixed feelings came over her. The horror of seeing Cory with a bloody gunshot wound to the head at the dining room table, mingled with memories of his loving touch and soft kisses.

"Oh, Maggie, I'm so sorry," Jess said, giving her a hug. "Go ahead and cry, it's all right. When you're ready to go back to the house, I'll go with you."

When the crying spell eased, Maggie pulled away from Jess to get a tissue from the bathroom. "I'm sorry, Jess."

"No apology needed," Jess said. "Let's go enjoy the beach."

They walked down the steps to the first floor and past Mr. Zimmerman's office. They were about to go out the door leading toward the lake when the door to apartment 12C opened. An older woman with a green scarf tied around her head stopped in her tracks when she saw them, causing the thin wood tip cigar almost to fall from between her lips.

Based on how the wrinkled woman was dressed in a long gypsy skirt, moccasins and beaded necklaces, along with the fact that the woman's apartment was right below hers, she realized it had to be Ethel, the seer.

"You must be Ethel," Maggie said, smiling; hoping her eyes did not appear too red from crying. "I'm Maggie

and this is my friend, Jess. I just moved in, my apartment is right above you."

The woman seemed nervous, or else she had Parkinson's disease. Her hand quivered when she reached up to take the cigar from her mouth. "Yes, I'm Ethel. I'm surprised Mr. Zimmerman told you about me."

"It wasn't Mr. Zimmerman," Maggie said, moving the wine glasses to one hand. "It was Debbie on the second floor."

The old woman coughed, hacked, and coughed some more. "I'm sorry, I need a drink," she said, closing the door.

Maggie and Jess looked at each other and then walked out the door onto the wraparound porch. They walked down the steps, into the tall uncut grass, and up to the ridge of the bluff.

"Gee, Maggie," Jess said, stepping away from the weed-covered cliff. "That's a long way down there."

Maggie did not venture any closer. "I wouldn't want to live here if I had kids, they'd fall right off the edge."

They followed the ridge until they came up to a worn wooden landing. The steps, moss-covered and wet, followed the face of the clay bluff from small platform to small platform. Overgrown trees and shrubs obscured their view to the base of the stairway.

"Is it safe to go down these steps?" Jess asked, moving the rail back and forth. "This isn't even sturdy."

"Mr. Zimmerman didn't say anything about it," Maggie said, stepping gingerly onto the top step. "It feels okay."

"I'm going to need this wine when we get down there," Jess said, staying a few steps behind Maggie as they descended to the lake. "If we get there alive."

Maggie carefully tested each old board before placing her full weight onto it. Sometimes there was a spring in the boards, sometimes a snap. "I'm going to ask Mr. Zimmerman if there's a better way to get down there. This is freaking me out."

"I can't believe we're doing this," Jess said.

When they reached the first landing, Maggie looked down toward the sandy beach, up to where they had just come, and then at Jess. "You can come down here."

"I'm not standing on that with you," Jess said, shaking her head. "It might not support both of us."

Maggie laughed. "Okay, let's hurry up and get this over with."

After what seemed like an unacceptably long time, they finally reached solid ground. Jess fell to her knees as if she had just stepped off an airplane that had crash-landed.

They took off their shoes and walked through the deep, soft sand toward the lake. When they reached the water, the sand was wet and firm from the lapping waves. They could walk without taking two steps forward and one step back.

"This is nice," Maggie said, looking out over the whitecaps that were racing in to cover her feet, only to be pulled back into the Great Lake's vast body of water.

Jess looked back at the stairway. "Take your shoes with you; I want to find another way back up there."

They walked down the secluded beach. If it were not for the gulls, they would be the only ones on the lakeshore. As they walked along, drinking wine, they would occasionally stop to pick up stones. Brown lightning stones with patterned white cracks and smoothed, colorful beach glass caught their attention.

Some stones were flat, perfect for skipping over the water. While others found a home in their pockets.

When they came up to a large piece of driftwood, they sat down on it and looked back down the beach.

"That sanatorium is even eerier looking from this angle," Jess said, refilling her glass. "It reminds me of those old scary movies where there's a haunted castle on a cliff by the ocean, and there are thunder and lightning and huge waves crashing on boulders."

"It's not anything like that," Maggie said, nudging Jess with her elbow in jest. "And it's not a sanatorium anymore, it's called Sandpiper Bluff."

Maggie and Jess sat on the log for a while. They talked and laughed until their wine was nearly gone. The sun slowly dropped toward the horizon as the few distant clouds began to turn a peachy rose color.

"We'd better get back," Maggie said, standing. She wobbled and then caught her balance.

Jess looked further down the beach for a way to get back to the top of the bluff. She sighed. "Oh, great. We're going to have to go back up those steps because it's still quite a ways before the cliff tapers down."

They walked back to the dilapidated stairway, taking their time climbing to the top landing. When they reached the very top, they stood there looking at the building.

"It looks dark except for that Ethel's place," Jess said, holding the empty wine bottle.

"I don't think I told you that Ethel is a fortuneteller, at least that's what Debbie told me," Maggie said.

"No kidding," Jess said. She looked at Maggie and then back toward Maggie's apartment windows. "I think .

. ."

"You think what?" Maggie asked, looking at Jess's wide-open eyes.

"I must be seeing things," Jess said. She cleared her throat. "But I thought I saw someone walk past your window. I mean, it looked like someone was in your apartment. Did you lock the door?"

Maggie thought a moment. She reached into her pocket. Her fingers moved past the sandy stones she had collected and pulled out the brass skeleton key. The entrance key dangling from it, held in place by a twist tie she had taken from a loaf of bread. "I closed the door, but I didn't test it to see if it locked automatically."

"You've got to be kidding, Maggie," Jess said. "The superintendent gave you a skeleton key? Let me see it."

Maggie handed Jess the lever lock key.

"Do you know what a skeleton key is?" Jess asked as she examined it.

Maggie shrugged. "No, just some old antique key." "Skeleton keys are master keys," Jess said, handing it back to Maggie. "You have a key that can open any lock in the place. This key is probably from when the building was first built or when it was converted to a psychiatric hospital. The charge nurse probably had a skeleton key to lock patients in their rooms, and to let patients out of their rooms."

"Does that mean my key can open Debbie and Bruce's doors?" Maggie asked, shoving it back into her pocket.

"Probably," Jess said, looking back toward Maggie's room.

"Why would Mr. Zimmerman give me a master key?" Jess raised her eyebrows. "I hope he didn't give one to Debbie and Bruce. If he did, maybe one of them is in your room."

"Or," Maggie said, walking back toward the porch. "Maybe you're drunk and seeing things."

Jess did not answer as they trudged through lawn that was as much weeds as it was grass. When they stepped onto the porch, she tried the door. It was locked. "Can you unlock this?"

Maggie used the entrance key to open the door. The remaining warm rays of sunlight flooded the interior of Sandpiper Bluff, filling the previously unseen plaster cracks, causing them to look like rust-colored veins.

They walked inside and up the stairway to Maggie's apartment. Standing in front of the door, they listened. There were no sounds of anyone moving around on the other side of the door. Maggie turned the doorknob, the unlocked door opened.

"Must be I have to manually lock the door," Maggie said, pushing it all the way open.

Jess followed Maggie into the apartment, closing the door behind her. The room felt damp and chilly. With a quiet slowness, they looked through the rooms for an intruder or anything missing. Everything was fine.

"Jess," Maggie said, in a somewhat pleading voice. "Can you stay with me tonight? There's a spare room."

Jess did not say anything as she looked into the spare bedroom.

Maggie noticed Jess's hesitation. There was no way she was staying there alone when Jess thought she saw someone inside the apartment. "You've been drinking. You know you're not supposed to drink and drive. Besides, I'd feel awful and never forgive myself if I let you drive and something happened to you." She walked into the kitchen where Jess had sat her purse on the table. "Are your car keys in your purse?"

Jess sighed. "Okay, you win. I'll spend the night."

FIVE

JESS AWOKE FROM a fitful sleep. It took a few seconds for her to realize that she was not home in her nice cozy bed, but instead inside Maggie's haunted apartment building. She lay on her side in the dark, looking at the closed bedroom door. All she heard was the distant drip of a faucet. Might as well get up, get a drink, and use the bathroom, she thought.

She pushed the stale-smelling sheet aside and sat on the edge of the bed, waiting for her eyes to adjust to the darkness. She stood and walked toward the door. When she opened it, a sense of dread came over her. What was it about this place? Oh, yeah, it is haunted, she thought to herself.

With only a T-shirt and underpants on, she walked into the living room. Diffuse white light from the landscape filtered into the apartment from the full moon hidden from view.

The oven light, left on for a nightlight, guided Jess's path into the kitchen. She turned on the water faucet and rinsed the glass she had used to drink wine. The water sputtered as pockets of air escaped from the pipes. She

found the kitchen light, turned it on, and noticed the water had a rusty color to it when she filled her glass. I am not drinking that; she muttered as he dumped out the water and took a can of pop out of the refrigerator.

The moon reflecting on the calm lake drew her attention as she walked back into the living room. It reminded her of the Vincent van Gogh painting *Starry Night over the Rhone*. While she stood there, looking out the window, she heard a noise in the hallway.

Letting her curiosity get the best of her, she quietly walked to the door and looked out the peephole. The hallway was dark, except for a small amount of light that rose through the stairwell from the floor below.

Was someone walking around out there? It was hard to tell, she could not see enough to make out anything. She stepped away from the door and was about to go to the bathroom when it sounded like someone touched the doorknob on the other side. Jess froze, paralyzed by fear. The door was locked; they had made sure of that before they went to sleep. But there was no deadbolt or chain lock. If someone had a skeleton key like Maggie's, he or she would be able to walk right in.

Part of Jess wanted to run up, fling the door open, and surprise whoever was on the other side. But the other part of Jess was afraid of who, or what, may be there. She stared at the doorknob and when there were no further attempts to turn it, she ran into Maggie's room.

"Maggie," Jess whispered as she shook her shoulder. "Maggie, wake up."

Maggie opened her eyes and looked at the clock on the end table. "Jess, it's three in the morning. What's going on?"

"Someone was just trying to get in your front door," Jess said, turning on Maggie's bedroom light.

"What?" Maggie rubbed her eyes. "Are you sure?

Maybe you were dreaming."

"I wasn't dreaming," Jess said, holding up the can of pop still in her trembling hand. "I was drinking this wide awake, not in my sleep."

Maggie was alarmed. Who wanted to come into her apartment in the middle of the night? They walked into the living room and looked at the door. Silence.

"I'm afraid to look out the peephole," Maggie said, crossing her arms from the chill in the air. "Someone might be looking back at me."

"I looked through it earlier," Jess whispered. "It's too dark out there to see anything."

Then they heard a door close.

"That sounded like it came from Debbie's apartment," Maggie said, looking at Jess.

"You should have Mr. Zimmerman put another lock on your door," Jess said. She looked around the sparsely furnished living room for something heavy to push in front of the door, to keep whoever was trying to break in, from getting inside. "We should put something in front of the door, at least until you get another lock."

"The couch is the only thing," Maggie said, walking to one end of an old, worn Florence Knoll Sofa. "Help me push it."

They tugged on the long, midcentury couch. Its metal legs pulled on the rust-orange shag carpet until it was pressed against the wooden door.

"I feel a little safer," Maggie said, walking back to her room.

"I don't," Jess said, closing her bedroom door.

SIX

JESS HAD ALREADY showered and dressed by the time Maggie got up. She walked into the kitchen where Jess was finishing a cup of coffee.

"It's been a blast, Maggie," Jess said sarcastically. "But I need to get out of here. Do you want to come with me?"

Maggie laughed. "There has to be a logical explanation for what happened last night."

"Like what?"

"Like maybe Debbie came home drunk and forgot which apartment was hers."

Jess sat her cup in the sink. "Terrible explanation, I don't buy it. What else do you have?"

Maggie filled her cup with coffee and looked at Jess. "Your imagination ran away with you? You know how you think this place is haunted, and every little thing is a ghost."

"Nope, that's not it," Jess said, shaking her head. She picked up her purse and walked toward the couch still blocking the door. "It's quite possible there are crazy people living in this place; you said they seemed a little odd."

Maggie helped Jess move the sofa so she could escape, pushing the old heavy piece of furniture across the carpet with a dull rumble.

"You babysit tonight?" Jess asked as she walked toward the door.

"Yep," Maggie said, rolling her eyes. "I can't believe I got myself into that one."

"I'd get out of it if I were you," Jess said. She looked toward the living room windows. "You might consider locking your windows because that porch is right there. Anyone could walk right up to them and get inside."

Maggie looked at the windows and then back at Jess. "I'll suffocate. There's no air conditioning."

Jess's hand rested on the doorknob. "Don't take any more babysitting jobs. That Debbie seems a little weird to me, and I haven't even met her."

Maggie sighed.

"I think you should go back to your house. I know you don't want to live there because of the suicide, but at least it's safe." Jess opened the door and stepped over the threshold. Even though the sun outside was bright, its yellow rays turned a murky gray as they formed shadows against the walls. She shivered. "I'll call you tomorrow."

Maggie closed and locked the door. Jess was right; this place was creepy, but not creepy enough to move.

She walked to the kitchen and refilled her coffee cup. Outside, the calm lake reflected the blue sky and appeared refreshing. But inside Maggie's apartment it felt damp, and the air smelled musty. She opened a window to let in the clean air. A fan would help circulate the air, she thought. She would have to get one the next time she went to town.

Maggie walked out of her apartment and around the hall corner to the door leading out to the second floor wraparound porch. She put her coffee cup in the other hand and pushed down the French door handle to open it. The door was stuck. Not necessarily from swollen, summer wood, but more likely from not having been opened in a while.

She used her body to push the door open, spilling a couple drops of coffee onto the wood floor in the process. The warm, pine-scented breeze made the hair framing her face tickle her cheeks as if it wanted her to stay outside and play. She pushed the hair behind her ears and walked in front of her apartment windows. Anyone standing here could look right inside her living room. Not very private, she thought. When she looked closer at the loose-fitting window screens, she realized they would be easy to remove or at least kick in to gain entry. But who would do that? The only people with access to the porch are the people who live here.

She looked toward the section of the porch in front of Bruce's apartment, wondering why he had not taken the time to put a chair outside his windows to enjoy the summer sun. Maybe he was not the outdoor type.

Maggie walked around the corner of the porch, to the north side of the building, in front of the bedroom windows. This expanse also led to a small diamond-shaped window in front of the stairway.

She walked to the cushion-sized window and looked through it. Her apartment door was closed. She would have fainted if she saw it was open when she knew she had closed it. Thanks, Jess, for making me a nervous wreck.

Maggie turned away and walked to the northeast corner of the porch. She stood there, not going any farther because Debbie's apartment would be facing this part of the wraparound. She would not continue exploring.

Looking out to the parking lot, she saw her car, an old, rusted Lincoln, and another old gray sedan. She guessed the Lincoln belonged to Mr. Zimmerman.

She looked up to the third floor; there was no porch above her, only the superintendent's residence. Looking back down the length of the porch on the east side of the building she noticed another small diamond-shaped window next to the stairway, another set of French doors, and then Debbie's windows.

She walked past the stairway window and was about to open the door leading back inside when she heard voices coming from Debbie's apartment.

She did not want to listen and invade her privacy, but as she pushed the resistant door, a couple words said with a harsh whisper caught her attention. "Not tonight, later. There is time to complete the task . . . She has no idea what lies ahead."

Maggie stopped pushing on the door, not wanting to draw attention to herself. She took her hand off the handle and walked back around to the other door. When she opened it, it scraped along the hardwood floor. She had made so much noise opening and closing it, she just knew Debbie had to be looking at her through her door's peephole.

Acting as though she had not heard the person speaking in Debbie's apartment, she casually walked to her apartment, went inside, and closed the door.

Who was talking with that witchy voice? That did not sound like Debbie and certainly not Susie; or was it

something entirely different? It was just a whisper. Maybe a grandparent was visiting. Gee, I'm getting paranoid, Maggie said to herself. Get back to work.

She walked into the kitchen, took a black trash bag from the drawer, and walked into the spare room where Jess had slept. Doing the mundane task of laundry would get her mind off

Debbie and the possible intruder. Since Susie would be sleeping in this bed later tonight, the sheets needed to be washed anyway.

The washer and dryer were in the basement, at least that is what Mr. Zimmerman told her. Since she did not yet have a laundry basket, she stuffed the sheets and pillowcases into the bag, grabbed a pocketful of quarters, a container of laundry detergent, and walked out the door.

Thinking about what Jess had said about someone trying to get into the apartment, she took the skeleton key and locked the door from the outside before walking past the utility room to the elevator. She walked inside and pressed the button with a big black B on it. As the elevator began closing, she noticed Debbie's door open, but the door clanked shut before she could see who was coming out.

She watched the numbers light up as the elevator descended. It was so slow, she felt like it would have been faster to walk down the stairs.

The elevator jolted to a stop and the door rattled open, revealing a dark corridor with flickering fluorescent overhead lights. The scent of musk and of a dead animal, probably a mouse, made her wonder if she would have been better off going to a Laundromat.

SEVEN

MAGGIE ADJUSTED THE bag of dirty clothes and held it at her side as she stepped off the elevator and into the dimly lit basement. She knew the washer and dryer were down here, but Mr. Zimmerman had not shown them to her when she came to see the apartment and sign the lease.

She looked down at the dirty concrete floor. Moisture oozed from the corner where the dingy white painted concrete walls met the floor. Looking up, she saw old fluorescent lights flickering and heard them hum a continuous noise down the length of the long corridor.

To the left was the stairway and to the right was an open door to a dark room. Thinking it could be the laundry room; she reached inside and felt for a light switch. Finally finding the switch, she flipped it on. A light bulb hanging from an electrical cord came on, revealing boxes, bins, and items that seemed to be in storage. When she looked farther back into the space, she noticed hospital beds, old-fashioned wheelchairs, and stretchers. The reminders of the building's history made her shiver. She wondered how many people had died there.

She turned the light off and continued down the hallway. There were two other rooms on the right, but she was not able to open them. Good, they are locked, she thought. She really did not want to see what might be inside them.

The room in the left corner of the basement had a dim nightlight. She could see a washing machine and a dryer inside. Relieved, she walked into the room.

She turned on another flickering fluorescent lamp, causing its electromagnetic ballast to emit a headache producing buzz. She sat the bag of sheets and detergent on the small table and looked inside the only washing machine. It looked clean enough, so she put the required quarters into the slots, pushed in the coin slide, and pressed start.

When she had finished loading the washer, she closed the lid, took the garbage bag, and walked back into the hall. Between the noise and the smell, there was no way she was going to sit in the room and wait for the wash to finish. Instead of taking the elevator, she decided she would take the stairs back up to the second floor; at least they were open and spacious.

When she got to the lobby, she saw Ethel come in through the front door.

"Hi, Ethel," Maggie said, rounding the corner to continue her ascent.

"Hi, dear," Ethel said, with vocal cords made of sandpaper. "Sorry about yesterday, but I had a coughing spell and had to take care of it. I get those every now and then."

"Not a problem," Maggie said, standing on the next flight of stairs. She noticed Ethel had stopped and was staring at her as if she had seen something frightful. "Is everything okay?"

"Yes, dear," Ethel said, waving her hand in front of her face. "I sometimes get spells. I'm fine."

"Spells?" Maggie questioned. "Like a seizure?" Ethel nodded. "Yes, like that, but not a seizure."

"I hope you feel better," Maggie said, concerned for the elderly woman. "Is there anything I can do?"

"Thank you, but I'm fine," Ethel said. She began walking toward her apartment and then stopped. She turned and looked back at Maggie, who had continued her climb. "Dear?"

Maggie stopped and turned to look at Ethel. "Yes?"

"I hope you don't think I'm strange, but I'm able to see into the future and I would love to read you sometime. Would that be all right?"

Maggie shrugged. She did not necessarily believe in that kind of thing, but she agreed. "Sure, sounds like fun."

"Can we make it soon?" Ethel asked, stroking the beads around her neck.

Her expression was so serious that Maggie was beginning to think Ethel was seeing something that very moment. She nodded and continued up the stairway as Ethel stood there, watching her.

That was strange, she thought, as she continued climbing. When she reached the second floor, she stood there and listened. It was quiet, too quiet.

When she reached her apartment door, she turned the knob, making sure it was still locked. Thankfully, it was. She took the key from her pocket, unlocked the door, and walked inside. After closing the door, she locked it with her skeleton key.

"I've got to call Mr. Zimmerman and get another lock on this door," she said to herself.

She looked at the black rotary telephone sitting on one of the end tables in the living room. Sandpiper Bluff was located too far away from a telephone company to get the internet through the phone line so she would not bother connecting the old phone. Her cell phone would work fine connecting to the World Wide Web. Especially since the apartments had no cable or satellite hookups.

A portable black-and-white television set was on the other table. It could not be used either because there was no digital converter box.

Furnished apartment? Yeah, right, Maggie thought as she took her cell phone off the kitchen table. She called Mr. Zimmerman, but it rang and rang, not allowing her a way to leave a message. She would try again later.

It would be several hours before Debbie brought Susie over for her to babysit. In the meantime, Maggie finished the wash, made chocolate chip cookies, and worked on book four of the Raven's Ridge Mysteries.

EIGHT

SHORTLY AFTER TEN o'clock, a cold gust of wind blew in through the apartment windows, causing Maggie to shiver. She stopped typing and got up from the dinette table where she had been working the last few hours and went to close the windows. When she had finished pulling down the final window sash, there was a knock on the door. That must be Debbie, she thought.

Before unlocking the door, she looked through the peephole. Just as expected, Debbie and Susie were standing on the other side.

She opened the door and welcomed them inside. Debbie was wearing a white nurse dress; she even had a nurse cap pinned to her pulled up hair. Maggie did not think nurses even wore those antiquated nursing clothes anymore. She was used to seeing nurses in colorful scrubs.

"Thank you for watching Susie," Debbie said, smiling. "If I don't have to work overtime, I'll be back around eight in the morning."

"Sure, not a problem," Maggie said, looking at Susie, who was already dressed in a long white nightgown. She

held a brown teddy bear in her hand. "Hi Susie, how are you? Do you like chocolate chip cookies?"

Susie kept looking at the floor and shrugged.

"She's a little shy," Debbie said in her usual bubbly manner. "She'll warm up to you though."

"That's fine," Maggie said.

"Oh, I have to go," Debbie said, looking at her watch. "She's already eaten and it's her bedtime. Should be an easy night for you."

"I'm sure it will be."

Debbie gave Susie a hug and walked out the door. "See ya."

"Have a good night at work," Maggie called after her. Then she locked the door and knelt down next to Susie. She looked at the matted fur on the stuffed animal she clutched in her hand. "I like your teddy bear; does he have a name?"

Susie shrugged as she looked at her bear and then with big sad eyes, she looked up at Maggie.

"I'll show you around," Maggie said, reaching for Susie's hand. But Susie held tight to the teddy with two hands. It did not surprise Maggie that Susie was not ready to warm up to her, she had only met Maggie one time, and that was for a few minutes in the hallway. "That's all right, this place isn't a palace."

When she had finished pointing out the bathroom, her bedroom, and the kitchen, she said, "Your mom said it was your bedtime. Are you ready to be tucked in or do you want to stay up a little while longer?"

Susie yawned.

"I think that means bedtime," Maggie said, walking to Susie's room.

Susie watched her and then followed her into the small room. She climbed into bed and turned to face the window.

Maggie tucked her in. "Good night. I'll be right next door if you need anything."

She turned off Susie's light and kept the bedroom door halfway open. Then she walked into the kitchen and sat in front of her computer to continue working on her novel. So far, this babysitting job is not so bad, she thought. There were no kids running around, screaming, and getting into things. Susie was the complete opposite.

Maggie forced herself to type but after half an hour of forcing the words out, she decided to get ready for bed. She wanted to get up early and be awake and dressed when Debbie arrived to pick up Susie.

She put on her pajamas and peeked into Susie's room; she was sound asleep. Then she walked into her room, leaving the door partway open, and got into bed. She pulled the sheet up around her shoulders and closed her eyes. The building did indeed do a lot of groaning and creaking, just as Mr. Zimmerman had told her. Sometimes it sounded like there was activity in the hallway, at other times it seemed like someone was riding the elevator up to the third floor and then down to the basement. Who would be doing that at this time of night? Fortunately, those sounds were outside Maggie's apartment where they were not a threat.

She rolled over and finally went to sleep. Time passed until something startled her awake. She looked at the clock; it was around three in the morning. She lay still and listened. The elevator was moving. Maybe it was Bruce coming home from the bar, she thought. Despite the fact, she had no idea if Bruce even drank.

Maggie kept listening. It sounded as if several people had come off the elevator and were whispering in the hallway. Then fear rushed through her, it sounded as though someone had turned her doorknob. She quietly rolled over, faced her door, and screamed. Susie was standing in her bedroom doorway, standing there and staring at her. She had not expected that.

"Susie, come here," Maggie said, wanting Susie with her, just in case someone was trying to break in.

Susie stood there, oblivious to what Maggie was saying. Maggie jumped out of bed and put her arms around Susie and listened. There were no further sounds, either of her doorknob or out in the hallway. She was definitely getting a deadbolt even if she had to buy and install it herself.

"You're cold," Maggie said, feeling an icy chill radiate from Susie. "Are you feeling okay?"

Susie did not answer; she just stared ahead as if she was sleepwalking.

"Let's get you back to bed," Maggie said, directing Susie back to her room. She tucked her in, even teddy. She brushed Susie's stringy hair off her forehead and walked into the living room.

Maggie looked through the door's peephole and saw nothing. Deciding to follow Jess's suggestion, she pushed the couch in front of the door. After struggling with the heavy piece of furniture, she finally had the Florence Knoll blocking the entry.

NINE

MAGGIE HAD THE couch moved away from the door where it had acted as a barricade during the early morning hours. Now it sat unusually close to the door, but Maggie did not care. She knew that if she did not get a better lock on the door she would have to use it again tonight. If she had a skeleton key, that would most likely open the other doors on the floor, who else was in possession of one. She would ask Mr. Zimmerman about the key if she could ever get a hold of him to ask the question.

Susie sat across from Maggie at the small kitchen table, not touching her cereal or milk. Instead, she held her dirty-looking teddy bear, smoothing its ratty synthetic fur.

"Aren't you hungry?" Maggie asked, looking up from her manuscript.

Susie shrugged, not making eye contact with her.

Maggie looked at the bowl of soon to be soggy corn flakes. "Do you want sugar on your cereal? That's how I eat mine."

Before Susie answered, there was a knock on the door.

"That must be your mom," Maggie said as she stood up to answer the door. She looked through the peephole and saw Debbie with her back toward the door. Even though she could not see her face, she could tell it was Debbie by the white cap, so she opened the door.

Debbie stood at the door with a big smile. Her face looked drawn and pale, bust she was still full of spunk. "There's my little pumpkin."

Maggie turned around and saw Susie standing right behind her, twisting and pulling the teddy bear's head as if she were wringing its neck. Maggie was speechless for a moment because Susie was petting the poor little stuffed animal a few moments ago, and now she seemed to want teddy dead. The behavior caught her off guard. Then she said, "I don't think Susie felt well last night. She was standing at my bedroom door and was cold. I mean, she actually felt cold, but she seems better this morning."

"She gets that way sometimes," Debbie said, holding out her hand for Susie to come her way. "Nothing to worry about."

Maggie did not say anything as Susie walked past her to Debbie's open hand. "Oh, one more thing, before you go. I thought I heard people in the hallway and using the elevator last night. Does that happen very often?"

Debbie shook her head, dismissing Maggie's question. "Probably Bruce; sometimes he has a party in his pad." Debbie squinted. "But you should avoid the man. Sure, Bruce can be a nice guy, but he and I . . . Well, we kind of have a thing together. We're tight if you know what I mean."

Maggie nodded, but she was not sure what Debbie was talking about. Were they romantically involved? She

was curious but did not figure it was her business to know all about Debbie's affairs, or lack thereof.

"Later," Debbie said as she and Susie scurried away.

No sooner had Maggie closed the door and locked it with her skeleton key when the cell phone rang. It was Jess.

"Hey, Maggie, how was your night babysitting?" "It was fine. Susie slept most of the night." "What about noises?"

Maggie cleared her throat. "I did hear people and what sounded like someone turning my doorknob, but Debbie said Bruce sometimes has parties, so I'm assuming that's what I heard."

"Maybe," Jess said with uncertainty. She paused and then said, "I know you probably don't want to do this, but I think we should go back to your house and get things squared away. It's been over a month."

Immediately, images of Cory dead on the floor, blood pooled around his head, and the gun at his side made her queasy. She did not want to go back there. After the police had given the okay, Jess and a couple of other friends had cleaned the house, wiping the blood from the tile floor and making it look as though nothing had happened. But what still needed to be done was to go through papers and find insurance policies, bank statements, stocks certificates, and to get the will from the safe so that the estate could be settled. Maggie did not want to think about financial details but knew she had to do it.

"I suppose." Maggie sighed.

"Great, I'll pick you up around noon."

TEN

"I'M STOPPING AT Lenny's," Jess said. She slowed the car and pulled into the grocery store's parking lot. "You're going to need something strong to drink to get through this."

"Liquor?" Maggie frowned and looked at Jess as she pulled into a parking spot and turned off the car. "I suppose you're right, but I'll probably start bawling anyway once I start going through our things."

"It'll make you feel better." "It'll make me feel hung over."

Maggie and Jess walked into the store and up to the speedy checkout where the lottery tickets and liquor were kept. Jess bought a bottle of bourbon whiskey, while Maggie bought one instant lottery ticket.

"Big spender," Jess said, picking up the brown paper bag with the bourbon inside.

"It only takes one to win." Maggie put the ticket into her purse.

When they were walking out of the store, the old woman who was standing behind Maggie in the checkout lane a few days earlier was walking inside the store. She was hunched over and walked with shuffling steps. When the woman looked up and noticed Maggie, she tipped to the side and into a movie rental machine.

"Are you all right?" Maggie asked, reaching over to keep her from falling.

The old woman adjusted her shawl and her thick-lensed glasses. With cloudy cataract eyes, she looked straight at Maggie. "It is you," she said, surprised at their meeting. "I may not see well, but I can tell you have something attached to you."

"Yes, we met the other day standing in line," Maggie said, backing up. She decided to ignore her comment about something being attached to her.

"Have you left that old sanatorium yet?"

Wow, what is it with no one wanting her to live there? "No, I'm settling in."

"I wouldn't settle in if I were you." The woman then looked at Jess, who was still standing where she had stopped when Maggie ran up to help the woman. "And you, girly, over there. I don't . . . I don't like . . ."

Jess began walking out the door, ignoring the old woman. "Maggie, come on."

Maggie watched Jess walk toward the car and then looked at the woman. "We haven't been introduced, my name is Margaret McGee."

"I'm Claudia," she said as people moved past them. She motioned for Maggie to come closer. "I don't usually tell people things I see, but I feel you are in danger and that you need to move out of that old hospital and get new friends."

"I don't understand. How do you know this?" Maggie said, her face was only inches from the woman's wrinkled skin.

"I was born with a gift, the gift of healing," the woman said, tapping her cane on the slip-resistant flooring. "Some call it a curse, especially since it took my health. But I can see things most people can't." Then seeming like she was becoming annoyed with the conversation she began shuffling away. In the same whiny voice she had used while putting the cantaloupe and prune juice on the checkout conveyor belt a few days earlier, she belted out, "Just trust me!"

Maggie watched the woman continue inside the store. What in the world was that about? Moving out of her apartment was beginning to sound like a good idea, but leaving Jess? Jess was her best friend and she trusted her with her life. Maggie turned and walked back out to the car where Jess was waiting.

"Who was that old bag," Jess said, backing out of the parking spot.

Maggie pulled the seatbelt across her body and latched it. "I met her a few days ago when I was getting groceries. She's just concerned."

"She's crazy." Jess floored the car, causing its wheels to spray loose gravel at the car behind her.

Maggie laughed. "I'm beginning to think everyone's crazy."

ELEVEN

AFTER DRIVING FOR an hour, Jess pulled into the driveway of Maggie's two-story colonial home just outside the Breedsville city limits. She turned the ignition off and they sat there, staring at the house.

Jess looked over at Maggie. "Are you ready to go in?"

Maggie was surprised her hands were trembling as she took the house keys from her purse. "No, I'm not ready. I'm totally dreading this."

"Do you know where all the paperwork is that you need?"

"It should be in Cory's office in the file cabinet or in the safe."

Jess's hand rested on top of the whiskey's brown paper sack. "Do you remember how to get into the safe?"

"Yeah." Maggie nodded. "I haven't been in it for a while, but unless the combination was changed, I should be able to get into it."

Jess pulled the whiskey out of the sack and held it up. "Do you want a swig of this before we go inside?"

"Nah," Maggie said, opening the car door. "Let's get this over with."

Jess held the bottle as they walked up the brick steps to the front door. Maggie unlocked the door but was afraid to open it.

"Are you going inside?" Jess asked.

Maggie put her hand on the brass knob, turned it, and pushed the door open. Jess walked past her and into the foyer.

"It's okay, Maggie. You can come in."

Maggie stepped onto the rug and stopped. She looked into the living room, then toward the stairway, and finally into the dining room. The oak table had it chairs pushed neatly into place. A vase with artificial daffodils sat on a doily in the center of the tabletop. Then she looked at the floor. It was clean. Actually, the house looked like it was ready to be shown by a realtor during an open house. Nevertheless, images of Cory's dead, crumpled body flashed through her mind. She could still see the red blood on the slate tile floor. The handgun that was at his side was the one that they kept locked inside the safe. At least it looked like their gun. The police had the gun now.

"Are you okay?" Jess asked, noticing she was looking at the suicide scene.

Maggie looked at Jess and nodded. "Yeah, I'm fine.

You guys did a nice job cleaning the house."

"Anything to help," Jess said, walking past the dining room table and into the kitchen as if nothing had ever happened. She retrieved two tumblers from the cupboard and put ice cubes into each. "Does ice get stale?" she asked, walking back to the foyer.

"Probably," Maggie said, taking the glass that Jess handed her.

"What the hell." Jess smiled and poured the bourbon over the ice. She raised her glass to propose a toast. "To

our dear Cory: May you be in heaven fifteen minutes before the devil knows you are dead."

"Hear, hear."

They clinked glasses, drank down the woody liquor, and then walked past the stairs to Cory's office.

Tears welled up in Maggie's eyes when she saw the picture of her and Cory at the Grand Canyon. It was sitting on his desk next to the round glass paperweight with an American Staffordshire inside. She had gotten it for him on his birthday last year. She wiped the tears from her eyes with the side of her hand.

Jess gave her a hug. "It's okay, everything will be all right."

Maggie took a tissue from a box sitting on top of a worktable and dabbed the moisture around here puffy eyes. After she had shoved the tissue into her pocket, she walked over to the file cabinet. Even though Cory owned a construction company, he should have been an accountant because he kept meticulous records. Files were in alphabetical order and color-coded. She pulled open the second drawer and found the folder labeled INSURANCE and pulled it out from behind the folder labeled INCIDENTS.

She sat at the desk and opened the folder. The auto, homeowners, and life insurance policies were inside. Maggie pulled out the life insurance policy and looked for the section on coverage for suicide cases. "Hmm, I'm not sure if the policy has coverage for suicide or not. It says that bodily injury that is the result of willful or malicious acts of the insured or is intended by the insured is excluded from coverage."

"Take it to a lawyer," Jess said as she moved around the room, looking inside cabinets and drawers.

"Yeah, I will." Maggie looked up from the policy and watched Jess open a cigar box filled with miscellaneous items instead of cigars. "What are you looking for?"

Jess closed the lid. "Nothing. Just being nosy, I guess."

Maggie drummed her fingers on the large desk pad calendar. "What else am I looking for?"

"The will?" Jess immediately answered.

"Oh, yeah." Maggie stood and walked to the bookcase built into the far wall.

"I thought the will was in a safe," Jess said, watching Maggie as she began taking books off the center shelf.

Maggie took George Orwell's *1984* off the shelf and sat it gently on the floor beside her. Then J. R. R. Tolkien's trilogy of *The Lord of the Rings* was next. When she finally removed an oil painting that had been cut to fit behind the books, and between the shelves, sitting flush against the wall, a previously hidden wall safe was revealed.

"Good hiding place," Jess said, moving up behind Maggie.

Maggie punched in a code on the keypad and the small wall safe opened, revealing two narrow shelves. The lower shelf used to hold the handgun that Cory used to commit suicide, now only a box of ammunition sat there. The other shelf had an envelope, an old coin, and jewelry. "Is that coin and jewelry valuable?" Jess asked,

moving in for a closer look.

Maggie took out the envelope. "They belonged to Cory's grandmother. She was wealthy and passed them down to Cory."

"What about Cory's parents, did they get anything?" "They got a lot," Maggie said, opening the envelope

to make sure the will was inside it. "But his Oma Gerdie,

that's what he called her, didn't entirely trust that his parents would pass down any of their wealth to him. I disagree, however, because they dote on him and give him whatever he wants." Maggie looked up from the envelope. "I mean gave him . . ."

"It'll get easier," Jess said softly.

Maggie took a deep breath and read the beginning of the document. "Last will and testament of Cory McGee." She sighed and placed it gently back inside the envelope. "I'll take this to the lawyer, too."

"Were there any changes to it?"

"Changes?" Maggie asked, closing the safe. "Why do you ask?"

"It's always good to know those things."

Maggie replaced the picture in front of the safe and began re-shelving the books. When she had finished, she sat back down at Cory's desk. "I could use another shot of that whiskey."

"I'll get us more ice," Jess said, leaving the office.

Maggie leaned forward and began reading Cory's entries on the calendar while she waited for Jess to return. A meeting with a client had been scheduled for yesterday; a hair appointment for this Monday and a note to call JP. Who was JP? Cory's crew foreman was named Jim Peterman; it could be him. But then, Maggie did not know all the people that Cory had dealings with.

"Here you go," Jess said, walking into the room. She sat the tumbler of ice and bourbon on the desk next to the calendar. "Drink up."

Maggie downed the contents of the glass; it felt both cold and hot in her mouth. "You know

Jess, I don't usually drink whiskey, but I guess I have a good excuse today."

"Yes, you do." Jess had taken a seat in the chair in front of the desk, facing Maggie. She sat her empty glass on the desktop.

"You're not going to be able to drive." Maggie waved her hand in front of her face, trying to catch the bit of air it moved, to cool her now flushed face. She looked back down at the calendar and looked at the date he had taken his life, May first. There was only one note jotted into the box, it simply said JP. Surely the police had noticed this and followed up on it. Maggie still could not believe Cory could take his own life. Someone else had to be involved, but the police seemed not to agree. His death was caused by a self-inflicted gunshot wound, there was no evidence to the contrary.

"We'll just stay here tonight," Jess said, leaning forward. She put her elbows on the desk and asked, "What are you looking at?"

"Oh, nothing." Maggie leaned back in the cushioned chair. For the moment, she was happy.

"Let's play some music," Jess said, looking at the small radio on top of the file cabinet. "Do you mind if I play music on the audio system in the living room? It'll sound better than that radio up there."

"Sure, but I'm not going into that part of the house," Maggie said, closing her eyes.

Jess picked up Maggie's glass and walked into the living room.

Maggie was surprised that Jess chose classical music. She had never heard her listen to anything other than rock or pop. Still curious about JP, Maggie flipped the page of the calendar to April. She found one JP and then another.

"I brought you another drink." Jess sat it beside Maggie along with the whiskey bottle. "Still looking at that calendar?"

Maggie shrugged and reached for the tumbler. She was feeling the whiskey's effect on her senses, or rather lack of senses, as she downed the drink. Then she looked at Jess's empty tumbler. "Your glass is empty." Maggie was beginning to slur her speech.

"I already drank it," Jess said.

"Is that Bach you're playing?" Maggie's elbow slipped off the table.

"It is the Goldberg Variations; do you like it?"

"I didn't even know we had it," Maggie said. "It sounds beautiful, though."

Jess reached over and filled Maggie's glass.

"No more," Maggie said, reaching for Jess's hand.

Jess continued pouring. "I don't want you to get all depressed on me, being here in the house and all. Besides, it's Saturday, and I want to have some fun."

The whiskey had taken Maggie's common sense and thrown it out the window for the buzzards to peck at like roadkill and carry away. "One more, then. I don't want to go all crazy on you."

Jess filled the glass and sat back in the chair on the other side of the desk. "Maggie, you know you can call me anytime if you need anything. I know this is hard for you, losing Cory, but I will always be here for you."

With words that smeared into each other, she said, "I know Jess; you're my best friend in the entire world. If I can't depend on you, who can I depend on?"

Jess smiled and watched as Maggie tipped to the side and almost fell out of the chair. "I still think you should move out of that awful apartment building. It's so old and

rundown, not to mention it has a spooky history. I wouldn't be surprised if someone died there. Actually, I'm sure people died there because it was a hospital."

The whiskey was going down like cherry Kool-Aid. So much so that when she set the glass back down, it tipped over. Jess jumped up and ran to the kitchen, returning with a dishtowel.

"I think it's time for bed," Jess said, drying the desktop.

Maggie tried to stand but slid to her knees, giggling. "But I don't want to go to bed; I'm having fun. Isn't that what you wanted?"

"To your feet," Jess said, helping her stand. She guided her to the downstairs guest room where she fell onto the bed. Jess took off Maggie's shoes and covered her with the blanket that had been folded at the foot of the bed. "Sweet dreams," she said, closing the bedroom door tight as she left the room.

TWELVE

"I'M NEVER DRINKING again," Maggie said, adjusting the sunglasses she had borrowed from Jess. "And thanks for letting me use these shades. My eyes are rather sensitive today."

Jess laughed as she pulled up to the sidewalk leading to the entry of Sandpiper Bluff. "I take it you're not going to church this morning, and no problem, you can keep them. I have another pair I like better, anyway." Jess looked at the building and cringed. "Do you want me to go in with you?"

Maggie opened the car door and got out. "That won't be necessary."

Jess waved as she drove away. Maggie felt woozy as she walked up to the double doors and inside the vestibule. She decided to look into the cloudy window of her mailbox to see if there was any mail in it, but as expected there was not. She unlocked the door and went inside the building. Glancing over at the superintendent's office, she hoped to see Mr. Zimmerman so that she could ask about getting a better lock for her apartment door, but he was not there.

Other than the sound of her shoes scuffing on the steps as she walked up to the second floor, the building was quiet. As she walked to her apartment, Bruce's door opened.

"Oh, hi, Maggie," Bruce said. He moved the garbage bag he was holding to his other hand and raised his eyebrows. "Do you feel okay?"

Maggie knew she looked awful. She had not showered, had bed head, and she still was wearing Jess's sunglasses. She stopped and looked at him. He wore a white T-shirt, blue denim jeans, and his black hair was swept neatly up from the forehead. She took the sunglasses off and smiled. "I'm fine, just had a little too much to drink last night."

"I have just the cure for that," he said, opening his door wider. "Come on in and I'll get you fixed up."

"That's all right, but I think I'll just go take a nap." Then she remembered she was out of aspirin. "You wouldn't happen to have any aspirin, would you?"

"I have a whole bottle of pills. Come inside and I'll get them for you."

Maggie thought she had to get to know the guy anyway, so she might as well follow him inside apartment 20A. She looked at his lock on the way inside; it looked the same as hers. "The

CONNIE MYRES

locks in this place are old; do you have to use a skeleton key?"

"No, not a skeleton key," he said, gesturing for Maggie to sit at the chrome dining table. His apartment was different from hers. The kitchen was the first room walked into; the living room was beyond that—it was larger than hers with south and west-facing windows—and the bathroom and bedroom were to the left.

Bruce walked to the bathroom and returned with a bottle of aspirin. He drew a glass of water and sat both the bottle and water in front of her on the Formica tabletop. Then he filled the teakettle with water and sat it on the stove's burner. "Chamomile tea with honey will cure that hangover of yours."

Maggie swallowed the aspirin. She did not want to stay, but he was already heating the water. "Maybe one cup."

He pulled out a turquoise vinyl-covered cushioned chair and sat at the table across from her. "Are you liking it here?"

No. "Yes, the place has great views. How about you?

Have you lived here long?"

He leaned back and crossed his muscular arms over his chest. "Yeah, I've been here a long time. It's hard to leave this place. Sure, Mr. Zimmerman could do a better job of maintaining it, but not a bad trade-off for living on a bluff overlooking Lake Michigan." He did not take his eyes off her. "So what do you do for a living?"

Maggie was beginning to feel a little uncomfortable with his fixed gaze. Or was it bedroom eyes. "I'm a writer."

"A writer, that's wonderful," he said, sounding interested. "I would have taken you for a nurse. You look so kind and empathetic, especially since you helped Debbie out by babysitting Susie. Not many people would have done that."

Maggie glanced at the steam coming out of the teakettle's spout and then looked at Bruce. "Good guess. I used to work as a nurse. And the babysitting," she shrugged. "Debbie needed help. What was I to do?"

"Debbie always has problems with finding someone to watch Susie, mostly because she can be a handful." Bruce leaned forward and put his elbows on the table. "I used to watch her, but I think she needs to be at a psychiatric hospital."

"Why is that?" Maggie thought there was something off about Susie, and Debbie for that matter.

"Because Susie has an antisocial personality disorder. You don't have a cat, bird, or some other animal, do you?" The teakettle's sharp whistle was increasing with

Maggie's anxiety. "No, but why?"

Bruce stood, took the angry kettle off the heat, and poured the boiling water over an infuser of chamomile inside the rose porcelain teapot. While the tea steeped, he said, "She has a history of being cruel to animals . . . Even people."

"What?" Maggie was shocked. How could Debbie ask her to babysit a child that should be institutionalized? "You have to be kidding."

Bruce took two matching teacups, spoons, and a honey pot with a wand to the table. "She's better now. Debbie makes sure she takes her medicine. There haven't been any negative episodes in a long time."

"How do you know all this?"

"I used to be her psychiatrist." Bruce removed the infuser from the teapot and poured them each a cup of steaming tea.

"Is it safe to babysit her?" Maggie watched Bruce drizzle honey into her cup of chamomile. Her throbbing head and queasy stomach were minor compared to the terror of having babysat someone who could be dangerous.

He sipped his tea. "It's safe."

Maggie looked at the light brown liquid in her cup. She stirred and took a sip, thinking there was no way she was babysitting again. The tea was warm and soothing. Maybe she was overreacting; Bruce did say she was better. "This is good."

Bruce reached across the table with an open hand, beckoning for a handhold. "Anything for you, neighbor."

Maggie looked at Bruce; he was attractive. She would play along and put her hand in his, but that would be the extent of any physical contact between them. No sooner had she felt his warm, strong hand, than the door opened. It was Debbie.

Debbie stopped in her tracks and looked at their hands. "Maggie! I wasn't expecting to see you here. What's going on?"

Bruce pulled his hand away. "Maggie wasn't feeling well, so I made her some of my special hangover medicine. What are you up to?"

Debbie finished walking inside and closed the door behind her. "Just came to see you."

Maggie could not help but notice Debbie's skimpy clothing. A tight T-shirt hugged her braless breasts while low-cut, short shorts showed her belly button. Maggie got the impression Debbie was there for more than a cup of tea. "I was just leaving."

"You don't need to leave on my account." Debbie walked over to Bruce and put a hand on his shoulder. "I may need a babysitter soon. Are you up for it?"

Babysit? "Ah . . ." Maggie stood up.

"I don't know yet, I'll let you know." Debbie moved behind Bruce, put her arms around his shoulders, and brought her head next to his so that they were cheek to cheek.

Maggie looked at Bruce, who was looking back at her with eyes that said, *I am interested in you.* When she looked at Debbie's eyes, they said, *He is mine. Stay away.*

THIRTEEN

MAGGIE TOOK A pillow from her bed and lay down on the couch. She closed her eyes and began tallying a mental account of the positives and negatives in her life. Positives included Jess, her apartment's gorgeous view, and . . ., she paused. She could not think of any more positives. The negatives included the creepy building and its history, Debbie, Susie, and probably Bruce. Of course, the death of Cory was a negative, but there was nothing she could do about that. Before she dozed off, she debated whether she should call Ethel, Mr. Zimmerman, the cashier and the old woman at Lenny's, a positive or a negative. They could go either way, she thought.

Her slumber was interrupted by the sound of a door slamming shut. Was it Bruce's? She looked at her watch; it was one in the afternoon.

After she took a shower and grabbed a Diet Pepsi from the refrigerator, she decided to walk downstairs and out to the backyard. When she walked by Ethel's door, she stopped. For a moment, she had thought about speaking with the seer; after all, Ethel did invite her to stop by her apartment. Instead, Maggie continued walking out to the back porch.

The air was fresh and invigorating. It was if she walked outside a bubble, a bubble filled with a suffocating oily liquid.

"Hi, dear."

Maggie turned and saw Ethel sitting in a rocking chair at the end of the porch. "Hi, Ethel. Out enjoying this beautiful day?"

"Yes, I suppose I am." She coughed and then lit a wood tip cigar. "Or to have a smoke."

Maggie laughed.

"Care to join me?" Ethel said with her sandpaper voice as she pointed to the rocking chair next to hers.

"Sure, I'd love to." Maggie walked down the creaky planks and sat in the creaky rocker.

"Are you doing all right?"

"It's taking a little getting used to living here." Maggie watched the wind gently ruffle Ethel's loose gypsy skirt. "I could use a new lock, but I can't get a hold of Mr. Zimmerman. Have you seen him?"

Ethel blew a puff of smoke and adjusted the green scarf wrapped around her head. "He's usually in his apartment on the third floor. You may have to just go up there."

Maggie nodded.

Ethel rolled the ashes into the ashtray sitting on the small table between the two rockers. "No one else will tell you, but I will. This place is not all that it seems."

"I know about the building's history, but that was then, and this is now."

"True, but sometimes then is now, and now is then." "I don't know what you mean."

Ethel rocked back and forth. Back and forth. "I wanted to tell you to watch that friend of yours. I get a bad feeling about her."

"You're not the first one that's told me that," Maggie said. "An old lady at the grocery store said the same thing."

Ethel laughed and coughed at the same time. "That must be Claudia. We go way back. When I was a receptionist here, back in the sixties, Claudia and I used to belong to a group called The Seers. We would have séances right here in the basement of this building during the sixties. We were quite powerful back then; now we're just a couple of old hags. I don't think she even knows I live here."

"What did you do in the séances?"

"We communicated with spirits," Ethel said, smiling as if recalling the memories were pleasurable. "Claudia and I would take turns being the medium in charge of the séance. People would come from all around to speak with their deceased loved ones or have us tell their future. We made quite a living helping people," Ethel puffed the cigar. "But we were not frauds, not our group."

"Do you still have séances in the basement?"

"No, absolutely not." Ethel's pleasant thoughts must have turned to bad memories because she stopped rocking, and the hand holding the wood tip quivered. "We innocently contacted something evil, something from Hell and have not held a séance since then . . . not anywhere."

"What happened?" Even though Maggie did not necessarily believe in the paranormal, her interest was piqued.

Ethel stared off into the distant blue horizon, where the lake blended with the sky. She took a deep breath and said, "We used a crystal ball back then. I still have it, but I don't touch it now. There would be anywhere from three to six people who would sit around a table in, what we called the scrying room, in the basement. This place was a psychiatric hospital back then. Claudia and I were good friends with the manager, mostly because we got into contact with his deceased wife, making him happy so he let us do the séances here . . . As long as we would contact spirits for him whenever he asked. So time went on, and all was well until . . . January of 1969. That was when something other than the dead relatives of clients came to us."

Ethel paused and then continued. "A couple came to us, wanting to speak with their deceased daughter who had died of influenza.

They were heartbroken and full of emotion because of their grief. Anyway, it was my turn to use the crystal ball. Claudia lit candles and dimmed the lights because it helped me go into a trance. I was having difficulty contacting the little girl, probably because she was in heaven—it is only when souls are in purgatory or are earthbound that I can communicate with them. Anyway, the couple was sobbing, almost out of control, so I went into a deeper level of trance, and that was when the crystal ball turned black, and I mean the blackest of black. An inky black that seemed to draw goodness toward it, absorb it, and then release evil in exchange."

Ethel's hand trembled so bad she dropped the cigar onto the deck's peeling paint. She picked it up, drew in a deep breath of cancer, and continued. "My hands were pushed away from it as I came out of the trance. The evil had taken over the crystal ball, and there was nothing I

could do about it. The couple stopped sobbing, began cursing at me, calling me a witch, and ran out of the room and the building. Claudia then put her hands on the crystal and began chanting positive, white spells, but the sinister spirit inside the ball shot out and into Claudia."

Maggie could tell the conversation was affecting Ethel because her tremors increased and she inhaled the cigar like a cigarette. "I'm sorry, but you don't have to talk about it if you don't want to."

Ethel looked at Maggie. "I want to talk about it. Not for me, but for you."

"For me?"

"Yes, because you live here, now, and I want you to be aware of its dark side . . . I think you were drawn here for some reason. A reason that I have not figured out, yet. I would need to use the crystal ball again to find out."

Maybe Ethel was not imagining things; this place was strange and felt strange. "If you don't mind talking about it, what happened to Claudia when the evil spirit went inside her?"

"Her eyes turned black, like coal stones pushed into the face of a snowman. When it left her, shortly after entering, her eyesight was never the same. Neither was this place. Anyone who worked here or was a patient here became strange and sinister. The manager began drinking heavily, the staff treated the patients like dogs, and the symptoms of the psych patients became worse. I remember one little girl who came here around that time. She had a mental illness that caused her to be calm one moment and suddenly grow angry and vicious the next. But the girl's violent nature became worse, so much so that she supposedly got hold of something sharp and killed an orderly. Then, because the staff was all messed

up, she accidentally died while in restraints. They closed this place later that year because of accusations of abuse by the staff toward the patients."

"That happened here?"

"It happened on the second floor. That's where they kept violent patients that needed to be locked up."

Maggie liked Sandpiper Bluff less and less. "Were you affected by that evil spirit?"

"Claudia and I have always used spells of protection, I still do."

"Why are you still living here? I would've moved out a long time ago after seeing all that."

"Look around," Ethel said, moving her hand in front of her like a skinny model showing off a new car. "The place is beautiful, no place like it around." She looked at Maggie and winked. "And the rent is cheap."

"Is that spirit still around?"

Ethel shrugged. "Like I said, I haven't used the crystal ball since, but I get feelings that it's still here. After they stopped using this place as a psych hospital, only Mr. Zimmerman and I have lived here. He was the maintenance man back then, pretty much still is. I taught him how to protect himself, spiritually. Then in 2010, it was bought and turned into apartments, but that ended a couple of years later when no one would live here because of ghosts . . . Now you're here."

Maggie sighed as she thought about the positive and negative list she had tallied in her mind earlier that day. Evil spirit to the negative list. After they had talked for a while longer, she stood up and stretched. "Well, thank you, Ethel, for the additional knowledge about this place." Not really. "But I'm going for a walk."

"I hope I didn't upset you," Ethel said, acting as though she wanted to continue talking about the séances and the building.

"No, not at all. It's good to know what's going on." But sometimes ignorance was bliss, she thought.

She stepped off the porch and walked along the bluff toward the rickety stairway leading to the beach. When she reached the topmost landing, she leaned against the wobbly rail and soaked in the warm sunshine from above, the sounds of waves, and the long mew calls of the gulls below.

Maggie turned and looked back at the old building. When she first arrived at the place the remodeling seemed recent, but the longer she stayed there, the more rundown it looked. Either Mr. Zimmerman was majorly slacking on his duties or the place had a mind of its own.

She looked up at the third floor windows, hoping to see Mr. Zimmerman moving around inside so that she could go up and ask about getting another lock for her apartment, but the windows were dark. Then she looked at her windows, hoping no one was inside her apartment. There was no movement. Good.

She smiled as her mind wandered back to the fun—if that was what a person would call it—her and Jess had last night. No, not fun, she thought. Tolerance or maybe a numbing of memories. Then she thought about the desk calendar and the initials JP. Maybe she should call Jim and ask about his meetings with Cory, but then, maybe not. Whoever JP was always seemed to show up when Maggie was not around.

Then the words of Ethel and Claudia flashed in her mind and the words warning about Jess. Jess Pinter. Maggie shook her head; no way did JP refer to Jess. What

reason would Jess have for going to see Cory? Either they were planning a surprise party for her or . . . Or Jess was sleeping with Cory.

FOURTEEN

MAGGIE HAD JUST finished getting ready for bed when there was a knock on her door. She walked to the door and looked out the peephole; it was Debbie and Susie. Oh my god, she wants me to babysit, Maggie thought as she pinched her eyes tight in disbelief. For a moment, she thought about not answering the door, but Debbie probably heard her walk up to it and knows she is looking out the peephole at them that very moment.

She opened the door, with a yawn and a tired look. "Hi, Debbie."

Debbie was dressed in a white nursing dress and was looking a little down. "I'm sorry to bother you, Maggie. It looks like you're ready for bed, but I have to be to work in half an hour, and there is no one to watch Susie. Do you mind watching her tonight? I've been trying to

CONNIE MYRES

find another babysitter, but I'm not having any luck."

Maggie was stuck; how could she say no. She looked at Susie in her nightgown and the ragged teddy bear. It was not so bad last time she babysat; maybe it will be the same tonight. All she had to do was ignore what Bruce told her yesterday about Susie needing to be

institutionalized. If Susie could become violent, wouldn't she be better with a man like Bruce watching her? She let out a slow breath. "Sure."

"Thank you so much, Maggie. I owe you one." Debbie bent over, kissed Susie, and was off down the stairs before Maggie knew what had happened.

"Come inside, Susie." Maggie opened the door, and Susie walked in.

Maggie thought about pushing the couch up against the door so that no one would be able to enter during the night—since she still did not have the lock fixed—but what if she needed to escape the apartment fast. With Susie's supposed history, a person never knows when they may need to run for their life. But then, who said Bruce was right? Maybe he did not know what he was talking about. She locked the door with the skeleton key and pushed the couch in front of it.

When she had finished, she turned around and saw the bathroom door closed. Susie must be inside, Maggie thought, so she walked into the guest room and turned down the blankets.

When she had finished, Susie came out of the bathroom and walked into the bedroom.

"Are you ready for bed?"

Susie held her teddy and crawled into bed. Maggie could not help but feel sorry for the child. There were no other kids to play with in the apartment building, but then, giving Debbie the benefit of the doubt, maybe she goes to a playgroup with other kids during the week. Maggie covered Susie and tucked her in. "Good night, Susie."

Susie did not say anything.

Maggie left Susie's door open a crack and walked into her bedroom. Now she had to decide whether to leave her

door open as she did last time, close it or close and lock it. She wanted to lock it, but what if Susie needed something. Dependable Maggie opted to close the door and leave it unlocked.

She placed her cell phone on the nightstand beside the bed; it would be easy to get to if she needed to call 911. When she got into bed, she turned facing the door. Having her back to the door was the same as having an arm or leg hang off the bed where a monster might grab it and pull her underneath. In this case, a small child with a knife would come in and hack her to death.

"Don't be ridiculous, Maggie," she whispered to herself as she closed her eyes.

FIFTEEN

"MARGARET, ARE YOU sleeping?"

Maggie opened her eyes. She was staring at the paperwork in a notebook. She looked closer, it was a patient's chart. "What?"

"You need to get off the night shift, you're just not cut out for it," a bubbly voice said.

Maggie looked up and saw Debbie, or someone who looked like Debbie, standing next to her in a hospital nurses' station. A rolling rack of blue charts with patient's names was before her, a desk with papers, a phone, and an intercom system was on top of the desk. She noticed a watch with a white band on her wrist. When she looked down, she saw she had a nursing dress on, complete with white nylons and white nursing shoes. When she looked at Debbie, she looked a little younger but just as spunky. "Debbie, what's going on?"

"Debbie?" She sat down at the desk in the chair beside Maggie. "Are you blitzed? Since when do you call me Debbie?"

Maggie was confused. Was she dreaming? A dream with Debbie in it? It is a nightmare about this place and

the crazy psych nurses that Ethel was telling her about. But it seemed so real like she was really a nurse in a hospital. Because of the reality of the moment, Maggie decided to play along. She looked at Debbie's name badge; it said, Deborah F., Registered Nurse. "Deborah, I'm sorry."

A ringing sound blared from the hallway. "I'll get that call light, you finish charting." Deborah stood and was off down the hallway in seconds.

"Hi, Margaret." A male voice said from behind her. Maggie turned and saw Bruce. But was it really

Bruce? He stood there in a white lab coat with the name Bruce Hancock, MD monogrammed on the left chest, and he was looking rather handsome. His dark hair was slicked back, and he was smiling at her, just as he was smiling at her in his apartment the other day.

"Cat got your tongue?" He sat down in the chair Deborah had just left. He reached over and took Maggie's hand into his. "Do you want to do it now? I have time."

Was he talking about what Maggie thought he was talking about? His hand felt warm and soothing.

Bruce moved in closer until they touched knees. With one leg between hers, he leaned in and whispered. "Come on, baby. I've been waiting for this. The room is empty."

Margaret was startled away from the thrill of the moment when a clipboard smacked against the counter. Debbie was on the other side. "What's going on, here?"

Bruce stood and leaned toward Deborah. He whispered softly. "The room's ready, babe. Are you ready?"

Deborah's mood mellowed as she moved her face close to his. "I have a couple things to do first, and then I'll meet you there in ten minutes."

"Make it quick." Bruce walked out of the nurses' station and toward the exit stairway.

"Not too quick," Deborah said, licking her upper lip.

Then she turned and went back down the hall.

Maggie stood up and ran her hands down the front of the prim uniform. It felt real enough. She walked out of the nurses' station and into the hallway. It looked almost like the second floor of Sandpiper Bluff. Then she gasped when she saw a plaque on the wall that read LAKE SHORE SANATORIUM AND PSYCHIATRIC HOSPITAL.

Deborah came up beside Maggie. "I'll be off the floor for a while, so I'll need you to watch my patients. Here's the charge nurse's ward passkey."

Maggie lost her breath when Deborah handed her a skeleton key. It looked just like her apartment key.

"I know you haven't worked here long, but I need you to be the charge nurse for a little while. That key opens all the doors on this floor, but you probably won't need to use it."

Maggie tried to hand the key back, but Debbie would not take it. "I can't do this."

"Yes, you can, Margaret." Debbie sounded angry. "You can and you will." She poked her index finger into Maggie's chest. "And stay away from Bruce, he's mine. Got it?"

Maggie got it, but she did not know exactly what she had.

SIXTEEN

MAGGIE OPENED HER eyes. Her bedroom door was open. Had she gotten up during the night to use the bathroom and forgotten to close it? She could not remember. After adjusting her pillow, she looked at the nightstand clock, it was seven-thirty. Oh, great, I cannot believe I slept this late, she thought. Debbie will be here soon to pick up Susie.

Then she rolled on her back to give herself a few more minutes of snooze time before she got up. That is when her elbow touched something. She froze. Something was in bed with her. Too terrified to turn her head toward it, she could tell there was a figure under the blanket next to her, a human figure. Susie, it had to be Susie.

Maggie did not breathe for a moment, not wanting to awaken whatever it was beside her. It was not moving. It was lying there like a dead body. It had to be Susie sleeping; she probably came into her room during the night because she was afraid. But it was so still and so quiet. She could feel coldness radiate from it and hear no breathing.

As Maggie saw it, in the slow-motion seconds of the moment, she had two choices, either turn her head to see who it was or jump out of bed. If she jumped out of bed, she would awaken it, but then she would no longer be next to it. If she turned her head to look at its face, she would know who it was; Susie, of course.

She convinced herself it was Susie, who else could it be? And she would know that it was a child and not an *it* or a *thing*. So with her eyes taking the lead, she turned her head slowly, very slowly to see it. First, she saw Susie's snarled hair lying over the shoulders, then she saw the face. It was Susie's face, and she was staring at Maggie with black, cloudy eyes that did not blink or even seem to focus. Was Susie sleeping with her eyes open?

Maggie jumped out of bed without thinking as adrenaline surged through her body like an accelerator pump spraying gasoline. Then, performing her nursing duty, she reached over and shook Susie's shoulder to see if she was alive. God forbid if she had to give mouth-to-mouth resuscitation. Maggie felt for a pulse on the side of Susie's icy neck. She was not feeling the heart pumping blood through the artery.

Then suddenly Susie pulled her teddy bear up to her chest and sat up. Maggie was so startled she thought she would collapse from shock and Susie would be reviving her.

"Susie, are you okay?" Maggie said, relieved Susie was alive but baffled as to why she was.

Susie shrugged.

Bang, bang, bang sounded from the apartment door. Maggie was startled as her heart fluttered in her chest. Why was Debbie knocking like someone pissed off?

"Stay right there, Susie. That must be your mom." Maggie went to the door, pushed the couch to the side, and looked out the peephole. It was Debbie, so she unlocked and opened the door. "Debbie, I think Susie needs to go to the hospital."

Debbie was not her usual bubbly self, but rather a tired shift worker. "What's going on?"

"Follow me." Maggie turned to walk toward the bedroom, almost running into Susie, who was standing directly behind her. "Oh, are you feeling better?"

Susie nodded.

"She's fine," Debbie said, holding out her hand for Susie to take. "Like I said before, she sometimes has spells."

"I don't know; I think this was more than a spell." Maggie watched as Susie took Debbie's hand, and they walked into the hall. "I'd feel better if she got checked out by a doctor."

Debbie did not answer as she walked to her apartment.

Maggie closed the door. What could she do? Report Debbie for possible child neglect?

But Susie was up walking and shook her head to the affirmative when asked if she was okay. Maggie did not want to cause trouble and besides, Susie was fine when she walked out the door and Debbie knows about her so-called spells.

Enough thinking about it, she thought. Might as well get a shower and do laundry. After she showered and dressed, she took the sheets off the beds and put them into a garbage bag since she still did not have a laundry basket. She was about to walk out the door when the cell phone on her nightstand rang.

It was Nora Bella. "How's that manuscript coming along?"

"It's coming along, don't worry." However, Maggie was worried because she was behind schedule.

"Can you send it to me by the end of the week?" Maggie hesitated answering. "Sure."

"You sound tired, are you okay?" Nora's speech slowed; she sounded as though she was actually concerned about Maggie more than the book.

Maggie shrugged for no one to see. "It has been a little hard adjusting to everything that's happened."

"If things are too difficult, I may be able to convince the publisher to postpone things a bit, but for now, let's stay on schedule, okay?"

Maggie rolled her eyes. "Sure."

"Awesome, I expect to see the draft in my inbox by Friday afternoon. Chop, chop."

When Nora hung up the phone, Maggie decided that she was self-publishing when the contract ended. No more pressure from a bossy agent and no more having her profits gobbled up by greedy publishers. She picked up the laundry and detergent to continue where she had left off.

This morning she decided she would take the elevator, once again, to the basement laundry room. She pushed the button and waited, listening to the motor grind as if the wire cables were being stressed to their breaking point. Maggie was about to walk away when the elevator door opened. Why not?

She walked inside and chose the basement for her destination. The dingy cab shuddered and then descended. It clanked to a stop, and the door slid open. She stepped into the dampness and began walking

toward the laundry room. When she walked past the storage room, she noticed the last room on the right, which was previously locked, was slightly ajar.

Maggie remembered Ethel's talk of holding séances in the old hospital's basement years ago. Could that be the room, the scrying room? Before looking inside, she would get her clothes washing and then see what was inside the room.

With the rhythmical sound of water swishing in the background, she walked to the partially opened door.

"Hello." You never know, someone could be inside.

There was no answer, so she reached inside and felt for a light switch. When she found it, she flipped it up and down. It did not work, so she opened the door as far as it would go so that the flickering fluorescent lights from the corridor would illuminate at least part of the room.

"This is the room," Maggie whispered as she stood in the doorway.

Inside the darkened room was a round table with spent candles in the center, their hardened wax had dripped onto their holders. There were wooden table chairs scattered about the room, some were lying on their side on the dark concrete floor. It was difficult to see, but on the far wall was a drape covering something similar to a painting hanging. Maggie wondered what could be underneath it. She needed more light. Next time she came down here, she would bring her phone to use as a flashlight.

Something touched Maggie's shoulder. She jumped and screamed. When she turned around, she saw Bruce standing behind her.

"Sorry, didn't mean to scare you." He smiled unapologetically. "What are you doing?"

Maggie walked out of the doorway and stood in the hall. "I'm doing laundry and thought I'd look around." She looked toward the room. "Do you know anything about that room?"

"That room?" He glanced at it and then back at Maggie. "Why? Did you want to go inside?"

"I was just curious." She crossed her arms. "The light doesn't work, so it's hard to see what's inside."

"Stay here," Bruce said. He walked into the laundry room and returned with a candle. He pulled a lighter from his pocket and lit it. The flame flickered. "Want to see?"

Maggie was not sure she wanted to go inside anymore. Bruce seemed a little too eager to show her around, but she had to know. "I'll be right behind you."

Bruce walked into the room. The candle's flame flared and grew larger, casting dancing shadows on the black painted walls.

When they walked up to the table, Maggie noticed the tabletop looked like a rounded Ouija board. Symbols of the zodiac were in the outermost perimeter circle, followed by the alphabet, numbers, more symbols, and ending with a pentagram in the center. "A Ouija board?"

"A witchboard." Bruce ran his fingers along the dusty board, leaving a two-finger trail behind.

"Does anyone still use this room?"

Bruce looked at Maggie and smiled, while the candle glowed on his face, casting shadows that gave the impression he had deep-set eyes. "People used to use it."

Maggie was not sure she should ask the next question, it was rather personal and none of her business, but she decided to ask it anyway. "Did you ever use it?"

"Once upon a time," he said. "Why? Do you want to use it?"

"No," Maggie said, shaking her head; remembering what Ethel had told her. But Ethel never said anything about a witchboard. She looked at the back wall and the object that hung from the wall with a purple velvet cloth draped over it. "What's behind that cloth?"

Bruce smiled at her and held the candle toward her. "Here, hold this."

Maggie took the candle and watched as Bruce removed the velvet drape, revealing a large oval mirror with the strangest frame she had ever seen. At first, she thought it was vines carved into the wood but on closer inspection, she realized they were snakes, snakes intertwined into a coiling mass around the mirror. Reflecting from the black glass was the image of her and Bruce. "What kind of mirror is that?"

"It's used for scrying," Bruce said, staring at the reflection. "Want to try it?"

Bruce knew too much about the sinister-looking things in this room. Snakes were not the same as vines, and a witchboard was not the same as a decorative tabletop. "I think I'd better get back to my laundry."

Bruce looked at her from the reflection and she looked back. He smiled at her, but she did not smile back. "Sometimes things are not what they seem to be, Maggie."

What was he talking about? "I don't know what you mean."

He talked to her through the reflection in the mirror. "Come closer, stand next to me."

The mirror was strange. It had a feel to it, a pull to it. She walked closer and stood next to Bruce. He put his arm around her and pulled her even closer. "Just look into the mirror. Let it take you away."

She would play along. She looked at Bruce's reflection; he was no longer looking at her but rather staring off into a void as if he were in a trance. She noticed her breathing increase as if she was becoming short of breath from a heaviness in the air. The reflections around the room looked like robed people moving about. Oh, how the eye can play tricks on the mind, she thought. But one shadow, one hooded shadow was standing still; it was not dancing about like the others. Oh my god, there is something standing behind us. She pulled away from Bruce and turned around. Then she looked back at the mirror. It was gone. "Bruce, I saw something standing behind us. Let's get out of here."

Bruce followed Maggie out of the room. "Did something scare you?"

Maggie could hear the washer still agitating. She wanted to take the laundry out of the washer and never go back down in the basement ever again. But what was she going to with a load of wet clothes? She walked quickly toward the stairs. "I thought I saw something standing behind us."

"I'm sorry," Bruce said, climbing the steps behind her. "But you did want to know about the room."

When they got to the second floor, Maggie turned around. "I'm sorry. I guess my imagination ran away with me."

"It's all right," he said. "Why don't you stop over for supper tonight, Debbie is going to be stopping by."

"Thanks, but I should get work done tonight. I'm terribly behind."

"You still have to eat, don't you?" He walked toward his apartment. "We eat around six, I'll be expecting you."

Maggie watched Bruce walk into his apartment and close the door. She then went into hers. Why can't I be better at saying no? Now he is expecting me for supper.

SEVENTEEN

SHE PICKED UP her cell phone and walked down to the basement to get her clothes. The lights flickered as usual as she walked down the corridor to the laundry room. When she looked at the scrying room, she was relieved the door was still closed. She did not want inadvertently to see inside. Could that black-robed person be what was scaring people out of this place when it was previously opened as apartments? Ridiculous, she thought, it was just her imagination and the fact she was looking into a mirror in a creepy room.

Maggie sat her phone on top of the washer and began taking her clothes out of the tub; she had decided she would take them to the Laundromat to dry them. No more coming down to this basement, she decided. While she was putting the damp clothes and sheets into the garbage bag she heard something drop, it sounded like a chair. Like someone had lifted it into the air and let go. Chills spread instantly throughout her body. She could not move; all she could do was listen. There were no further noises.

Maggie refocused and crammed her laundry into the bag, picked up the laundry detergent, and walked out of the room. She was unable to resist the urge to look toward the scrying room. When she did, she noticed the door was open. She ran. When she got to the stairway, she realized she had left her cell phone lying on top of the washer.

Shit. She sat the bag down and quietly began walking back toward the laundry room; she did not want to let anyone know she was coming back. When she reached the laundry room, she picked up the phone and stepped back out into the corridor. When she looked over at the open door of the scrying room, she saw something move inside and a lit candle on the witchboard table. Was it Bruce? Was it Ethel? She was not sticking around to find out. She sprinted down the corridor, grabbed the bag of laundry, and ran up the stairs.

When she got to the first floor, she slowed down and listened for something following her. Nothing was; she had made it to safety. She sat the bag by Mr. Zimmerman's office and went up to her apartment to get her purse and car keys. After getting her things, she tested the door, making sure it was locked before leaving.

She walked down to the lobby, retrieved her laundry, and walked out to her car.

As she drove down the driveway, she looked at Sandpiper Bluff through the rear-view mirror. The building's reflection in the small mirror seemed to be in disrepair as she drove away. The rear-view mirror was deceptive, she thought. But it sure felt good to be away from the place.

When she drove into the village of Black Water, she was relieved to see a hardware store next to the

Laundromat. While her laundry dried, she would go next door and get a lock, fan, and laundry basket.

The Laundromat was bright and cheery, just what Maggie needed. She dumped the wet clothes into a dryer and walked over to the hardware store to get what she needed while the clothes dried.

A bell jingled when she walked into the home improvement store. She walked past lawn and garden products to the aisle with locks. When she found the deadbolt locks, the kind she wanted, she realized she was not going to be able to install it without Mr. Zimmerman's help. Leaving the aisle empty-handed, she looked for a laundry basket and a small box fan. She found them a couple aisles over.

While she was walking toward the checkout counter, she noticed a department labeled LOCAL HISTORY. She walked over to it. Local history books, pictures, and souvenirs were displayed on shelves. She sat down the basket and fan when she saw a book with a picture on its cover that resembled Sandpiper Bluff. Its title said *History of Lake Shore Sanatorium and Psychiatric Hospital: Legends, Lore, and Myths*.

She picked up the paperback book and began skimming through it. The timeline began in 1899 when it was built as a sanatorium for people with tuberculosis and ran to 2012 when its life as an apartment building ended. She was definitely buying this book.

Maggie put the book in the basket with the small fan and walked up to the counter to pay for them. The old man at the cash register kept looking at her as he rung up her items.

"Forty-seven fifteen," he said. Then while Maggie paid, he asked. "Do you have family around here?"

"Not in this area," she said, feeling uncomfortable by his gawking.

"I don't mean to make you feel uncomfortable," the man said, rubbing his stubble beard, "but you look familiar to me . . . can't quite place it."

Maggie thanked him and walked back to the Laundromat. She put the fan and book into the car and took the basket inside to gather her dried clothes. The thought of going back to Sandpiper Bluff was bringing her down. Maybe she would need to look for somewhere else to live.

EIGHTEEN

MAGGIE KEPT LOOKING over at the local history book she bought from the hardware store earlier. She resisted the urge to pick it up while she worked on her novel. If she were not so far behind writing the manuscript, she would sit down with a cup of coffee and read it. But learning about the building's history and lore was going to have to wait. Especially when she had to go to Bruce's for supper shortly.

Maggie heard an apartment door open and close, and then another. Debbie must have just gone to Bruce's, she thought. She looked at the clock; it was almost six. Time to get ready and go.

She closed her laptop and took a bottle of wine from the refrigerator; she would use it as a host gift for Bruce and Debbie. She had no ribbon or wrapping paper for it but did it really matter?

Maggie walked toward the door, pausing in front of the full-length mirror. She looked at her reflection for only a moment, just long enough to check her appearance, and if someone was standing behind her. Things were fine.

Not bothering to lock the door behind her, she walked to Bruce's and knocked. Bruce opened the door while Debbie stood at his side.

"Come in," he said, motioning for her to enter. "I wasn't sure you'd come or not."

"I'm happy to be here, thanks for inviting me." Garage rock played softly in the background while the aroma of something cooking in the oven made her mouth water. "Smells good in here."

Debbie took the bottle of wine from Maggie and handed it to Bruce. "It's meatloaf. Bruce is the best cook around. He's a better cook than my mom was. Aren't you babe?"

Bruce opened the wine and poured it into three glasses. "How's that hangover?"

Maggie shook her head. "It's long gone. I'll have to remember your cure . . . If I ever need it again."

"Have a seat at the table, you two," Bruce said, pulling the pan of meat out of the oven.

"So Maggie, Bruce tells me he helped you out in the basement, earlier." Debbie's bubbly personality was only cooking at a simmer.

"Help me?" She sipped her wine. "He just showed me that room in the corner."

Bruce brought the meatloaf, mashed potatoes, bread, and butter to the table. "She thought she saw something."

Maggie was about to respond to Bruce's comment when Debbie said, "Blessing?"

"Sure thing," Bruce said, straightening his posture as he sat down.

Bruce and Debbie held hands and extended their hand to Maggie. She could not help but think about the witchboard table and séances. She took their hands.

Bruce cleared his throat and said, "Lord, we know without a doubt that you'll bless this food as we pig out."

"Amen," Debbie said, loudly.

Maggie looked at Debbie and then at Bruce, who was staring at her. She did not think that meal blessing was quite appropriate, especially since it seemed they made fun of it. And the way he was still holding her hand, not letting go, was a little disquieting.

"Dig in," Bruce said, finally releasing Maggie.

"How's your writing coming along?" Debbie asked as she spoke with a mouth full of meatloaf.

Maggie took another sip of wine. "Fine." She looked at Bruce who kept glancing at her between bites of meat and potatoes.

"Eat, Maggie," Bruce said. "You came here for supper, didn't you?"

Maggie nodded and put small portions onto her plate. Who knew what ingredients he used when making the loaf; it could have an eye of newt and toe of frog for all she knew, especially after how he acted in the scrying room. Then she realized Susie was not there. "Where's Susie?"

"She's sleeping in Bruce's bedroom," Debbie said, seeming unconcerned.

"Is she okay?" Maggie forced a bite of meatloaf into her mouth and down her throat.

Debbie frowned at Maggie. "What? Do you think I can't care for Susie?"

"No, absolutely not." Maggie was caught off guard by Debbie's reaction. "Sorry."

"Babe, she didn't mean anything," Bruce said, resting his hand on her arm. "No worries, it's all cool."

Debbie smiled and nodded. "No, I'm sorry. I'm going to check on her now."

When Debbie left, Bruce scooted over into her seat so that he was close to Maggie. He moved in so his legs touched hers, just like in the dream she had.

Maggie did not know what to do. Was he coming on to her, and with Debbie in the next room? How bizarre this whole situation was, she could not move.

He brought his face closer to hers and whispered, "I'd like you come over and visit me. I'd like to get to know you better . . . A lot better."

Then the table shook; Debbie had kicked it. "What's going on here?"

CONNIE MYRES

Bruce stood and walked to Debbie. He put his arms around her and whispered something to her. Something that Maggie could not hear. Then he left the room.

Debbie looked at Maggie with an expression close to a sneer. "Stay away from Bruce, he's mine. Got it?"

Once again, Maggie got it, but she did not know exactly what she had.

NINETEEN

MAGGIE TOOK A break from writing and brewed herself some coffee. Even though Nora wanted a draft of the manuscript within the next two days, she needed to rest her tired eyes for a little while. She focused on a distant sailboat rather than on the computer screen.

She looked out the kitchen window, toward the horizon where dark clouds billowed and were heading her way. A late afternoon thunderstorm was forming. She decided she had time to take a cup of coffee onto the porch and recharge so that she could get back to typing before the storm struck.

When the coffee stopped dripping, she took a cup of it outside and stood in front of her living room windows, leaning on the railing toward Lake Michigan. A cool breeze was picking up and felt refreshing. She smelled the

CONNIE MYRES

moisture in the air and heard distant rumbles of thunder.

"Some night, huh?" Debbie said, walking up next to her. She leaned against the railing and looked out toward the lake.

Maggie looked at her. "What do you mean?"

"You don't remember?" Debbie turned and faced Maggie, blinking her fake eyelashes. "You don't remember acting like a whore and physically abusing Susie? You even tried to tie her to the bed so that you and Bruce could get it on."

"That's not true." Maggie protested the absurd remarks. "Are you joking? If you are, it's not funny."

"No, I'm not joking. You were crocked. After the wine was finished, you got into Bruce's stash of whiskey." Debbie smiled. "You don't remember?"

Maggie could not believe what Debbie was saying. "After you told me to stay away from Bruce, I left. I went to my apartment and went to sleep."

Debbie looked back toward the storm. "Well, you must have had a blackout then because you did do all that. I had to get Susie out of Bruce's place before you hurt her."

"No way," Maggie said, staring at the side of Debbie's powdered face. "You're making it up."

"If I'm making it up, why did I find your underpants in Bruce's bedroom?" Debbie turned back to Maggie. "If you don't believe me, ask Bruce; he'll tell you."

This moment was not recharging Maggie's batteries so that she could get back to writing, but rather overcharging them and causing them to spark. "I'm going to do that right now." Maggie started walking toward the French doors.

"He's not there," Debbie shouted behind her. "And I thought you should know that I reported you to child protective services."

Maggie stopped dead in her tracks. "What? You're crazy." Her heart was pounding; she could not believe what was happening.

"I'm not crazy, you are." Debbie kept leaning on the railing, staring at the black thunderhead puffing up before them, smiling.

Maggie could tell Debbie was obtaining pleasure from the moment. So much so, she thought Debbie would do a victory dance. "Why are you doing this? You know I didn't do any of that."

Debbie turned her head toward Maggie, who was standing in front of the doors. "I know you did, and I can prove it."

"By a pair of underpants you found in Bruce's apartment? They're not mine. They're probably yours."

"Not only because of your underpants but by the bruises on Susie's wrists and ankles when you tied her to the bed. You probably did the same thing when you babysat her."

"Why are you doing this? You know I didn't do any of that." Maggie was feeling overwhelmed.

"I'm not doing it to you, Maggie." Debbie's smile turned sour. "You're doing it to yourself. You're jealous of me and Bruce . . . And you're losing it."

Maggie could not listen to any more of Debbie's false accusations. Why was she doing this? Debbie was the one that was jealous, not her. Maggie pulled open the stubborn French doors and walked immediately to Bruce's apartment door. She knocked. No answer. She knocked some more. Again, no answer.

"Like I said, he's not there," Debbie said, walking past Maggie to her apartment.

Maggie knocked one more time before giving up. She turned and walked to her door, then stopped. There, at the foot of her apartment door, was a pair of underpants. They looked like hers. She walked up to them and

nudged them with her foot; yes, they were hers. She picked them up. That Debbie had to of left them there, but she could not have gotten them from Bruce's apartment, she had to have come into her apartment. Of course, she probably had a skeleton key just like Maggie, and she was the one going inside her apartment.

Maggie picked up the underpants and went into her apartment, tossing them into the new laundry basket she had bought. Wind gushed through her open windows as the storm approached the bluff. Maggie closed the windows and sat on the couch. Lightning flashed, and thunder cracked, causing her to jump. The storm blotted out any light left in the sky, leaving her apartment dark and cold.

She began to weep. She could not believe what was happening. How could she prove she did not do any of the things Debbie was accusing her of doing? Especially if Bruce backed up Debbie's story.

The building shook from the thunderous vibrations. She had to sleep. If she slept, she would not have to think about what was happening. She lay down and closed her eyes.

TWENTY

MAGGIE HELD THE master key in her hand and watched Deborah as she pranced down the stairway to her clandestine meeting with Dr. Bruce. She was alone on the psychiatric floor. Her white nursing shoes squeaked as she walked out of the nurses' station and into the hallway. The layout was almost like the second floor of Sandpiper Bluff. The apartments had to be rooms for patients, violent patients according to Ethel.

What was she to do? This was a dream, after all. But it did not feel like a dream. The sky through the double doors flashed with light from the storm outside. She could feel the cold metal of the key and the heavy dampness in the air.

She crossed her arms and turned around in a circle to look at her surroundings. The plaster walls had cracks, but they were not as prominent as they were now. Now? Oddly, the dream felt like now but it was not the now she was living in. Where she was in the hospital could not be real because her memories were of Sandpiper Bluff Apartments and not of this. Not of this time. She had no

idea what she was supposed to do. Yes, she was a nurse, and she knew what nurses did, but not here, not now.

Maggie almost jumped, almost dropping the key when she heard a scream come from her apartment, or rather, from the locked patients' room. The person in the room screamed again, then the nurse call light lit above the door, and a bell began ringing.

What was she supposed to do? When was Deborah getting back on the floor? Maggie walked up to the door and slid the skeleton key into the lock. She turned it, opened the door, and stood there. She could not believe what she was seeing. Her apartment had three hospital beds in it; the kitchen and two small bedrooms were nonexistent.

The first hospital bed had a patient curled up in the fetal position. The second bed had a patient sitting up, clutching her hospital gown while pointing to the patient in bed three. Maggie looked and saw a young girl, lying face down on the bed and secured with five-point restraints. The girl's wrists, ankles, and chest were tied to the bed so that she could not move. Indeed, she was not moving.

"She's dead," the second patient said, shaking from fright. "I called for help. I called for help."

Maggie walked up to the girl and nudged her shoulder. "Are you okay?"

The girl did not move.

"Here name is Susan," the second patient said. "Call her Susan, please."

Susan? This dream is out of control. Maggie palpated for a carotid pulse and listened for breathing, there was none. She took Susan out of the restraints and turned her onto her back. Susan was dead.

"Help, Deborah, help me," Maggie yelled as she began chest compressions. Moments later Deborah and Dr. Bruce ran into the room.

"What did you do?" Deborah said, watching Maggie perform CPR.

Dr. Bruce took the stethoscope from his lab coat pocket. "Stop compressions while I listen." He listened to her heart and then said, "She has expired. For the record, it's three in the morning."

They three of them stood there staring at Susan. Maggie could not believe what she was looking at.

Susan was dead. Her ratty hair and urine soaked gown made her look pathetic. She felt sorry for Susan and her poor care.

"You killed her," Deborah said, sneering. She looked at Maggie and waited for her reaction.

"I did not kill her; I was helping her." Maggie could not believe Deborah was casting such an accusation at her. "I answered the call light and found her like this. I took her out of the restraints to perform CPR. She probably died from asphyxiation from being face down on the blanket and pillow."

"You were in charge, and you were the only person on the unit when she died," Deborah said, not taking her eyes off Maggie. "You are responsible."

"I didn't put her in five-point restraints on her belly. I found her like this." From Deborah's facial expression, Maggie could tell she was thinking of a comeback.

Dr. Bruce put the stethoscope back into his pocket. "It appears she died from asphyxiation; an autopsy will need to be done."

Deborah and Dr. Bruce walked out of the room. Maggie pushed Susan's hair away from her sad little face

and then looked at the patient who had called for help. "You saw what happened, didn't you?"

The patient put her face into her hands and shook her head. She kept repeating, "I see no evil, hear no evil, speak no evil. I see no evil, hear no evil, speak no evil."

Maggie walked out of the room and to the nurses' station where Deborah and Dr. Bruce were talking. They stopped when Maggie walked to the desk. "Where's Susan's chart?"

Even though this was a dream, she still wanted to chart the facts of the incident.

"I have it," Deborah said, holding the blue chart in her hands. "I need to call the coroner and the authorities." Maggie took a blank sheet of nurse's notes from a wall pocket and began charting. She knew Deborah would not tell the truth, and she needed to protect herself. Deborah stood and rubbed against Dr. Bruce seductively. "Your notes won't matter; we know what happened. You were negligent, and now a patient is dead.

That is what the record will reflect."

Maggie looked at Dr. Bruce. "You know that's not true, right?"

Dr. Bruce did not say anything while Deborah whispered into his ear. "I concur with Deborah and will chart it as such."

"You're kidding?" They were setting her up to take the fall for a death that happened while they were off the floor having sex. It was coming down to either them or her. Someone was going to be accused of negligence, lose their job, and defend themselves in court. And they were winning.

TWENTY-ONE

MAGGIE SAT STRAIGHT up on the couch, having been startled awake. She had slept from the time she laid down on the couch all the way until Thursday morning. She looked around her apartment; there were no hospital beds or patients. The dream was so real.

"I'm moving out," she said to herself. She walked to the kitchen, picked up her cell phone from the table, and called Mr. Zimmerman. As usual, the phone rang and rang, not even an answering machine picked up. "Maybe he's in his office."

Still depressed from the conversation with Debbie, she did not even bother to comb her hair or brush her teeth. When she walked past the underpants in the basket, it occurred to her that she could defend herself by setting up a hidden camera in her apartment. And the next time Debbie came in—Debbie had to be sneaking into her apartment—she would have video proof that Debbie was making her look crazy. They had a video camera at the house, and it was able to detect motion and begin recording. She would pick it up after she went to Mr. Zimmerman's office.

She put her phone in her purse and walked out of the apartment, locking the door behind her. She looked at Bruce's door. Should she see if he was home and clear this mess up? Not now, she decided.

When she reached the lobby, she could see through the windowed enclosure that Mr. Zimmerman was not in his office. Where was he, on vacation? She walked to the room and looked in; maybe there was a note on the door or his desk indicating there had been a family emergency, and he had to leave, but he would be back. There was no note.

She looked through the glass and noticed a framed black-and-white photograph of a fishing charter boat with the name Castaway painted on the stern. The watercraft reminded her of the S.S. Minnow from *Gilligan's Island*.

Noticing there was a person at the helm, she decided to get a closer look. Was it the Carl Zimmerman she knew or was it his father? She tried the door; it was unlocked. She walked up to the picture and examined it. The man did indeed resemble Mr. Zimmerman; however, he was tall and trim, not stubby and potbellied. She could tell the photograph had been taken a long time ago by the way it was faded and yellowed around the edges. Based on what Claudia ranted about at the grocery store last week, it had to be Mr. Zimmerman's father. She must have meant it was him that was drunk and killed a man out on the water in front of this horrid place.

"Maggie, what are you doing in Mr. Zimmerman's office?" Ethel asked, through the open door.

Maggie turned around. "I was just looking at this picture. Is that—"

"It's not good to be inside this office," Ethel said, interrupting Maggie's question. She motioned for Maggie to leave.

"Of course, I'm sorry." Maggie walked out and closed the door.

Ethel began walking to the vestibule. "I'd like to stay and chat, Maggie, but I need to get to the store and get some items I need. I'll talk to you later."

Maggie watched as Ethel rushed out the door and down the porch steps. I wonder what her hurry is, she thought as she walked to her, still empty, mailbox.

The drive to her house distracted her from Debbie's lies—at least for the moment—as her car hummed along the rain-soaked roads from the storm during the night. Now, however, the rising sun cast a warm, bright light over the road and into the car. She pulled down the sun visor as she drove into Black Water. She got a cup of coffee and continued her journey, feeling much better as she got further away from the crazies.

The coffee was gone when she drove into her driveway. Between the trauma of Cory's death and Debbie's false accusations, she was becoming numb to the emotional pain. She got out of the car and went into the house, forcing herself to look into the dining room. Only a slight flush of agony rushed through her. Her mind was blocking out the misery, making her desensitized to the pain. She was changing her mind about selling the house; maybe she should move back in. It made the most sense, after all. First, she had to catch Debbie in the act of framing her so that she had more than her words to fight the lies.

Maggie walked into the office and to the drawer containing the camcorder. She took it out, along with the charger, and stuffed it inside her purse. Then she looked around the room and the file cabinet next to her. She remembered the INCIDENTS folder. Out of curiosity, she slid open the file cabinet drawer and pulled out the folder, then sat at the desk and opened it.

Records of on-the-job injuries by employees were inside. She thumbed through them and stopped when she reached the last sheet of paper, it had Jess's name written on it. It had her listed as an associate accountant. Jess was not an accountant; she was a waitress at Flashers, a bar not far from their house.

Moreover, Jess was not taking any accounting classes, so why did Cory hire her and why had not Jess said anything to her?

She pulled the sheet of paper out for closer inspection. If he had hired her as an associate accountant, something must have happened for him to add her to the INCIDENTS folder. There was no mention of an actual incident, other than next to the date February 14, it said, "Met after work for drinks, Chalet, blackmail." Maggie did not have to think too hard to conclude that Cory was having an affair with Jess and that she was blackmailing him. No way, it has to mean something else, she thought. Then she remembered she was out of town at a book signing that night. Not hard to forget since it was Saint Valentine's Day.

Maggie closed the folder. Cory did not act as if he was with Jess; but, of course, when someone is having an affair, learning to cover it up would be the top priority. But what about the mention of blackmail? Was it possible that Jess was blackmailing Cory? Was Jess demanding money from him in exchange for not telling her about

their relationship? Maggie's emotions exploded as sadness overtook her. What else could happen?

She went back to the file cabinet and pulled out the folder with the bank statements for his business. Even though Cory had these records on his computer, he always printed them out so that he had another copy. Maggie went immediately to the February statement, looking for anything out of the ordinary. There were expenditures for equipment, supplies, employee wages, and an ATM withdrawal of five-hundred dollars. Then she could not believe what she saw on the next line, a debit for Swiss Chalet. Oh my god, I think that is a motel, she said.

Maggie turned on Cory's computer and did a search for Swiss Chalet. It was just as she expected. The next town over had it listed as a short-stay motel, in other words, a no-tell motel. Tears streamed from Maggie's eyes as she went through the statements looking for any other mysterious withdrawals. There was none.

She closed the file and sobbed. It was as though everything had been taken from her. She was alone; there was no one she could count on, no one she could trust.

Maggie stood up and went into the bathroom. She took a washcloth from the closet and ran it under cool water to wipe her face. There had to be a logical explanation, she thought. I mean, if Jess actually was blackmailing Cory, he was not taking money from the business or from their personal checking account, she would have known, if he were. Then it struck her, right between the eyes like a hatchet blade. The only other thing of value they had that Jess could want as payment to cover up the affair was . . . the jewelry . . . The jewelry and the coin in the wall safe.

She threw down the washcloth and ran back into the office. Without concern for 1984 and The Lord of the Rings, she frantically pushed them away from the safe, causing them to fall to the floor as she fumbled with the keypad. When she finally got the correct code entered, she opened the safe. It was empty. Oma Gerdie's jewelry and the coin were gone. Everything was gone, even the ammunition for the handgun.

TWENTY-TWO

MAGGIE WAS FURIOUS. Jess must have watched her enter the wall safe's security code when she was getting inside it to retrieve Cory's Last Will and Testament. She was standing right behind me, she could see everything I did, Maggie said to herself. And she kept pushing me to drink to the point I was sloshed and passed out in bed. Jess could have taken the jewelry and the coin that night while I was sleeping like a corpse. She stomped her foot. How could I be so foolish, so trusting?

"I'm calling her," she said rushing to her purse and the phone inside. She dialed Jess, but it went to voicemail. I need to stay calm and act like nothing is going on, she thought. "Hey, Jess, what are you up to? Give me a call. Bye."

Maggie picked up her purse and the box of tissue. She was about to leave to drive to

Jess's when she thought she had better call her lawyer, Darron Sugarman. She sat at Cory's desk, found the phone number, and called the lawyer's office.

"Sugarman, Chandler, and Page Law Offices," the woman said. "May I help you?"

"I'm Margaret McGee and I had dropped some paperwork off for Mr. Sugarman to look at," Maggie said, trying not to sound like she was crying. "Do you know if he's had time to look at it?"

"He's in the office right now; would you like me to transfer you?"

"Yes, thank you."

"Darron Sugarman, what can I do for you?" the lawyer said with a slow, baritone voice.

"This is Maggie McGee, and I was wondering if you have looked at the paperwork I dropped off concerning my deceased husband."

"Yes, I have." Papers shuffled in the background. "Did you have a specific question?"

"I guess first I'd like to know if life insurance covers his suicide."

"Sadly, it does not. Unless it can be proved that he was insane and not responsible for his actions, I'm afraid it is not covered."

Maggie was not sure if she should bring up the blackmailing, yet. "Was there anything unusual about the will?"

"You are the sole beneficiary of the property and estate, real, personal, and mixed, tangible and intangible including the business of McGee Construction Company, after all debt and expenses are paid." The attorney cleared his throat. "There is something unusual though."

"What do you mean?"

"Your deceased husband bequeathed all jewelry, and a coin inherited from his grandmother Gerdie Lavis to one named Jessica Jane Pinter. Items include a 3-carat Golconda diamond ring valued at $300,000; a 65-carat Morganite platinum diamond pendant with a 14K gold

omega necklace valued at $60,000; and an 1802 Proof Draped Bust Silver Dollar valued at—I hope you are sitting down—1.3 million dollars."

Maggie gasped, partly from the shock of having items of that staggering value in their safe and the fact that Jessica Jane Pinter was now the owner of them. She stammered. "No, no, I had no idea. I knew they were valuable, but I didn't know they were that valuable . . . Is the will legal?"

"It appears to be. His signature is notarized and appears in order."

Maggie jumped in. "I checked the safe this morning before I came here, and the jewelry and the coin are missing. The only person who would know the code to get into the safe is Jessica Pinter. I believe she stole them." "It appears they are legally hers," Attorney Sugarman said. "However, if what you say is correct, and she entered your home illegally, without your permission, with the intent of stealing the jewelry and the coin, it would constitute breaking and entering, as well as burglary. Do you have proof that Jessica Jane Pinter took

the valuables from the safe?"

Maggie thought a moment. "No, but she's the only one, that I'm aware of, that knew about them and would possibly know the combination."

"Are you at the house now?" "Yes, I am."

"Call the police and file a report."

"I will." Maggie was not sure whether to mention the hunch she had about Jess because blackmail sounded so crazy, but she did. "I think Jess was blackmailing Cory."

"Are you sure about that? What proof do you have?"

"I have a letter and a bank statement. I'll send a copy to you."

"We may need to contest the will," Attorney Sugarman said. "Keep in touch."

When they disconnected, Maggie called the police. While she waited for them to come out to the house, she brainstormed how she could get proof that Jess came into the house and got into the safe. All she had was circumstantial evidence.

TWENTY-THREE

AFTER THE POLICE had left the house, Maggie locked up and drove to Cedar Creek Trailer Park to confront Jess. The sun was high in the sky by the time Maggie turned into the park. Kids were riding bikes on the narrow-paved roads and seniors were sitting on their trailer decks enjoying the sunny day. When she approached Jess's trailer, she noticed her car was not in the driveway. She was stopping and knocking at the door anyway.

Maggie drove up to the steps and turned off the car. She reached into her purse and turned on her phone's voice recorder. Even though she had no idea if it was legal to record someone without his or her knowledge, she needed proof Jess was guilty.

She walked up to the door and knocked. There was no answer. Knowing Jess was not home, she thought about going into the trailer just to do a little investigating. Maybe she would get lucky and see the jewelry and coin sitting on the counter. She knew that was highly unlikely but worth a try. Looking around she saw no one watching, so she turned the doorknob; it was locked. She had a key to Jess's trailer just as Jess had a key to her

house. Then it occurred to her, is it considered breaking and entering when you have a key? Is she breaking and entering? Was Jess really breaking and entering? What about the permission aspect? Maggie sighed, without catching Jess red handed with the goods, it was probably useless pressing charges. Just as Maggie could say she was stopping to pick up something she had left in the trailer when she lived there; Jess could say she was checking to make sure things were all right at the house.

Maggie unlocked the door and pushed it open. She walked into the trailer and closed the door. The smell of cigarette smoke hung in the air. "Jess, are you here?"

Not hearing an answer, she walked further inside. The living room had empty beer cans sitting around, and the kitchen counter had an old piece of chocolate cake that was attracting a line of ants. So far, nothing looked like Jess had sold the valuables and was living the high life.

She walked to the bathroom and then to Jess's bedroom. Should she look in dresser drawers? It would be a definite invasion of privacy, but then, she did steal from Maggie and

CONNIE MYRES

have an affair with her husband. At least that is how things seemed to be.

The month that Maggie had lived with Jess, she had never went into her bedroom or looked through her things. Part of Maggie felt awful for thinking her friend was a slut and thief, but the evidence was there, at least in Maggie's eyes. She walked up to Jess's nightstand and slid open the small drawer. Inside were lip balm, hand lotion, a condom, and various insignificant things.

"What are you doing?" Jess said, from behind her. Maggie pushed the drawer closed and turned around.

She had not heard Jess come into the trailer, and now she was the one caught getting into personal items. She had to

think of something to say, and quick. "Oh, hi, Jess. I am . . ."

"Why were you looking at my stuff?"

Maggie could not tell if Jess was angry or just putting on a show. "I'm sorry. I left my pendant here and I was just looking for it. I thought maybe if you found it you may have put it in there for safe keeping." Not a bad lie, she thought.

"I haven't seen a pendant. What does it look like?"

Gosh, now I have to expand my lie. "It looks like a butterfly."

Jess shook her head and walked into the kitchen, taking a can of beer from the fridge. "Do you want one?"

"No, I have to get back to the apartment."

Jess snapped the can tab open, walked into the living room, and sat on the lumpy sofa, propping her feet on the coffee table. "I'll call you if I find the pendant."

Maggie was feeling bad. Jess was not acting like a guilty person. She sat in the stained brown velvet chair across from Jess. How was she going to ask questions without sounding accusative? "I just came from the house, and it looked like someone has been there since we were there. Did you go back to the house for some reason?"

Jess shook her head. "Not me."

"You, know . . . I was going through more of Cory's papers and found one that said you worked for him as an associate accountant. Is that true?"

Jess took another swallow of beer. "Yeah, he hired me to do basic filing and data entry, nothing that has much to do with being an accountant."

"I didn't know, why didn't you tell me?"

"I thought you knew; I thought Cory told you. Besides, I didn't work much, only a night or two a week. It was just to supplement my income from Flashers."

Okay, she is making sense. Should she ask about the Swiss Chalet and St. Valentine's Day? If she did not, she would be mad at herself for not getting answers to those questions. "I also saw something about the Swiss Chalet." She studied Jess's expression, but she did not detect a look of guilt. At least so far.

"Oh, that," Jess said, glancing toward the ceiling. "He was busy and wanted me to help him by getting you a bouquet from the flower shop next door. We met in the parking lot of the Swiss Chalet because it was bigger than the little one the flower shop had. Did you get the flowers?"

Maggie arrived home the next evening, and there was indeed a bouquet on the dining room table for her. It was a beautiful arrangement of red roses, tulips, and frilly white baby's breath. "Why did you meet in the parking lot? Why not just bring the flowers back to the house?"

"I was not going back to the house, I was staying in town for a while, and Cory was driving through, so we just met up."

Jess seemed calm and assured. Had she practiced the answers and already prepared for Maggie's inevitable questions? Maggie wanted to mention the missing jewelry and coin but did not want Jess hiding anything more than what she already had. "I talked to the lawyer today."

Jess flinched and took a double swallow. "Oh, yeah?

What did he have to say?"

"He said that Cory gave Jessica Jane Pinter his grandma's jewelry and coin." Maggie did not take her eyes off Jess.

"He did?" Jessica smiled and leaned forward. "You're kidding?"

"You didn't know about that?" Maggie noticed that Jess seemed surprised. Maybe the surprise came from her realizing that her blackmailing actually worked.

"No, I didn't." Jess finished the can of beer and walked into the kitchen to get another.

"Why would he give you his grandma's things and not me? Any idea?" Maggie did not like the way that Jess seemed preoccupied with her newfound wealth rather than wondering why Maggie, Cory's wife, had not inherited them.

"I don't know." Jess sat back down. "But the two of you have not been getting along. Sometimes when he's working late and you're gone on business, he tells me things."

Maggie was shocked. Jess had to have noticed her reaction. "What things?"

"I don't know if I should say."

"He's dead, you can say." Maggie wanted the answer. "He said you're gone a lot and he gets lonely, and that when you're home you're either busy writing or too tired for anything and then you go to straight to bed . . . to go

to sleep."

The tide was turning. By what Jess was saying, she was leading up to the affair. However, Maggie had no idea anything was wrong with her and Cory's relationship. "Please, explain further, Jess. Just say it."

Jess leaned back and smiled. "Well, he and I have always gotten along, and quite frankly I have always been attracted to him." She looked at Maggie. "I don't believe you knew that he was attracted to me. Did you?"

Maggie sat speechless.

"I didn't think so. But now that he's dead, like you said, I might as well say it because I think you do know now." Jess leaned back and gazed out the window as if she were dreaming. "One night I stopped by the house to see you, but you were gone on business, some book signing or something, but Cory was home. He invited me in and we had a few drinks. Actually, more than a few drinks. And what can I say, one thing led to another and we . . ." Jess looked at Maggie. "Do you want me to continue?"

Maggie got the picture. Jess was a traitor friend and Cory was a cheat. She nodded.

"Well, I won't give you all the details, but I will tell you that we made love. Actually, since I'm coming clean, we made love many times. I'm surprised you never picked up on it. By the look you're giving me, I can tell you did not know he was planning on divorcing you. He was taking a long time to tell you though. I guess he felt sorry for you."

This was one more blow to her senses. Jess had reached into her chest and pulled out Maggie's heart. She did not cry, she was too numb. But one more thing was bothering her—the suicide. She kept her cool and asked, "Do you know anything about the suicide? Why would Cory commit suicide?"

Jess raised her eyebrows in thought. "I don't know. I think he was torn between us and couldn't take it anymore."

Even though Maggie was numb, it did not dull her suspicion of Jess. If Jess could have an affair with Cory behind her back, maybe she knew more about Cory's death than she was saying, so decided to lie. "The police told me they think someone murdered Cory, that it wasn't suicide."

Jess had a change of state. "What?"

Maggie smiled inside, but not really. Jess may have had something to do with Cory's death, but that was absurd. Jess is not capable of murder. Maybe she hired someone. "I don't know any more than that."

Jess's calm demeanor returned. "Are you a suspect?"

What? How had Jess turned this around? Had she done something to make Maggie look suspicious? But, first of all, the police saying it could be murder was a lie. Was it true? Maybe Jess was capable of more evil than Maggie had imagined. She stood up. "I think I need to get back home."

Jess did not say anything until Maggie was closing the door.

"Have you seen a psychiatrist lately, Maggie?" What the hell, was everyone insane?

TWENTY-FOUR

THE SUN HAD dropped below the horizon by the time Maggie drove down the long road to Sandpiper Bluff Apartments. What once seemed like the perfect place to live, was now foreboding. The instant the building came into view, Maggie felt it looked more like the Lake Shore Sanatorium and Psychiatric Hospital from her nightmares, rather than the home of her dreams. It was now a place she did not want to be, let alone go inside and live.

Maggie parked and looked at her reflection in the car's rear-view mirror. Her red and puffy eyes made it clear she had been crying, so she looked inside her purse for the sunglasses she had borrowed from Jess. She could not find them so she got out of the car and walked into the building, hoping she would not see anyone.

When she entered the lobby, she looked over at Mr. Zimmerman's office, he still was not there. She continued up the stairs and was almost to her room when Bruce walked out of his apartment.

"Hi, Maggie," he said. He studied her face. "Are you okay?"

Maggie looked away from him and walked up to her door, putting the key in the lock. Then she thought she would ask him about what Debbie was accusing her of. She turned toward Bruce. "I talked to Debbie yesterday, and she was saying things about me that weren't true."

Bruce walked up to Maggie as if entertained. "Like what?"

Maggie cleared her throat. "Remember when we had dinner Tuesday night?"

"Sure, how could I forget?" He smiled, looked at her chest, and then back up to her eyes.

Maggie looked away. "Well, Debbie was saying that you and I . . . I mean, you remember me leaving after supper, right?"

Bruce continued to smile while he crossed his arms and leaned against the wall next to Maggie's door. "Sure, I remember you leaving after dinner, but not right after dinner."

Maggie looked at him and then looked away when he winked at her. "What do you mean not right after dinner?"

"You don't remember, do you?" Bruce laughed. "That doesn't surprise me since you were getting heavy into the booze." He paused.

"I'm taking it that you don't remember that you and I had a little hanky-panky." He moved close to her. "Debbie was frost when you and I went into the bedroom to get it on." He touched the side of her cheek. "You were a little rough with Susie. The little brat had it coming, though, but you surprised me when you tied her to the bed . . . And then you tied me to . . ."

Maggie pushed his hand away. "You're lying, just like Debbie. Why are the two of you making this stuff up?"

Bruce began walking toward the stairway. "I'm not making it up. You just don't remember."

Maggie hurried inside her apartment and closed the door. No way in hell did she do all that. Bruce and Debbie were doing this to her for a reason. But what reason? She had never done anything to them, she just moved into this hole for Christ's sake.

She reached into her purse and took out the camera and its charger. She looked around the room, trying to find a place she could put it so that when Debbie or Bruce came into her apartment, they would not notice it. The area was sparse of furnishings so she would need to create a hiding spot for it. There were no bookshelves with knickknacks or potted plants of ferns, so she decided to put it in the backpack so that the lens could see through the crack of the unzipped zipper. The hiding spot also had the added advantage of looking like it belonged there if someone happened to see it.

Maggie pushed the kitchen's dinette table a foot toward the dining room so that the camera would have a good view of the apartment door. After making sure there was plenty of drive space for any recordings, she plugged it in and made sure it was set to record automatically when it sensed motion in the living room and the front door.

Now what? Maggie said to herself as she looked around the disquieting apartment. She wanted to pack up and move out that very second, but she needed to collect evidence to show that the crazy neighbors were entering her apartment and framing her. For now, she would have to stay in *Hell House*.

TWENTY-FIVE

MAGGIE WOKE UP and sighed. It was Friday morning, and Nora Bella was expecting her to send the completed manuscript of Raven Ridge today. She was so far behind; there was no way she was going to get it done. When Nora calls, and she will, Maggie would just have to ask her for an extension. Nora will not be happy, but there was no other option.

She lay on her side staring at the poorly painted plaster wall. Fortunately, she did not have a nightmare last night. No dream of Nurse Deborah and Dr. Bruce Hancock, and no image of the psychiatric patient, Susan, bond barbarically to a hospital bed, and lying there dead. Then she realized that her bed, the bed she was sleeping in, was in the same location as Susie's—well, Susie's in the dream. The bed she was sleeping in looked like a hospital bed.

It was small in size and had old tubular head and footboards, but there were no side rails or a way to raise and lower the head of the bed. However, she did notice an unusual crease that ran across the center of the mattress as if someone had folded it in half. She ran her hand along the bottom sheet feeling the groove. Then she jumped out

of bed and stared at it. She brought a hand to her mouth and whispered, "Or the mattress could be creased from the head of the bed having been raised and repeatedly lowered, just like a hospital bed."

There was one way to find out. She took the cell phone from the nightstand, turned on its light, and got down on her hands and knees to look under the bed. There were holes in the scratched metal frame, just like ones that are used to tie restraints, and the frame was split so that the head and foot of the bed could be elevated. She went to the foot and noticed a mechanism that could have once held two hand cranks for making manual adjustments.

"No frickin' way!" she said, pushing the mattress off the bed. Through the frame, she could see the old inner workings of the hospital bed. "I've been sleeping in a hospital bed? I can't believe it."

Maggie went into the spare room and pushed the mattress to the side; the bed was the same as hers. She was horrified. "They have to be beds from when this place was a hospital.

This is ridiculous; I'm not sleeping in that bed again."

She walked into the living room and stood there. The bed she had been sleeping in must have been one from the building's days as a psychiatric hospital. It had worn brown paint around the restraint holes in the bed frame, likely from frequent use. "This place is disgusting."

While she made coffee, she thought about how a place with a warbler singing outside the window and a view of blue water and sky, could be so dark and freakish. Even the air inside the building was growing increasingly heavy, like walking through a film of some unseen substance.

She sneaked a cup of coffee as it dripped into the pot and took the camcorder from its hiding spot. Just as expected, the only recording was herself when she had set it and walked to her bedroom, and when she woke up and went into the living room. But to get the recording she needed, she would have to leave the apartment and give Debbie a chance to come in and do whatever she is going to do. For the first time since Cory's death, going back to the house and sleeping in their bed sounded comforting.

Her shoulders slumped when she looked at her laptop sitting across from the backpack. She had so much writing to do and did not feel like doing it. She was too distracted with all the other things going on in her life. Not to mention, Nora will be calling her soon to see if the manuscript was done and ready to email.

Maggie sat at the dinette table and found the recording she made of her and Jess yesterday. When she played it, all she could hear was static scratching over their voices. It was impossible to make anything out. "So much for that evidence," she said, putting it into her purse.

She finished her coffee, took a much overdue shower, and put her laptop into the backpack. Then she stuffed as much clothing as she could fit into it. She did not want to let Debbie know she was moving out by taking the suitcase. The apartment needed to look like she was living there even though she did not intend to spend much time there.

But what to do with the camcorder? She thought about putting it under the couch, but the view would not be optimal, not to mention the fact that Debbie would probably notice it. Then she looked into the bedrooms.

"Yes, that will work," she said, walking into her room. She put the mattress back on the bed, fluffed the sheet and blanket into a messy pile, and placed the camera inside, leaving a tiny opening for the lens to see out. She swung the bedroom door all the way open. The camera now had a view of the apartment door, but not further inside the apartment. But catching Debbie entering the apartment would be enough to prove she was setting up Maggie for something. But what?

When Maggie left and locked her apartment, she made enough noise so that Debbie would know she had left. Debbie's apartment faced the parking lot, so all she had to do was look out her window and see if Maggie's car was there or not. Nonetheless, she wanted to make it clear she was not in the apartment.

She was thankful she had not run into anyone on the way out to her car. Once again, it felt like a burden had been lifted from her shoulders as she drove away from the old sanatorium. If it were not for the new knowledge of Cory's affair with Jess, she would have felt blissful. Instead, she drove to her house in meditative silence.

When she reached the house, she checked the mailbox and went inside. Junk mail and a couple of bills were all there was. She looked toward the dining room table, there was still no way she could live in the house permanently, but for now, it was better than the apartment.

She walked past the table, into the kitchen, and opened the refrigerator door; all there was inside was bottled water, ketchup, and mustard. I'll order a pizza later, she thought. Then she walked into the office, moved Cory's computer to the side, and put her computer in its place so that she could get some work done.

Then her cell phone rang, it was Nora Bella. "Hi, Nora."

"Just checking to see if you mailed the manuscript, I don't see it in my inbox."

Maggie leaned back in the chair. "I'm working on it right now, but I'm going to need more time."

"How much time?"

Maggie had no idea how much time—lots of time. "Next week."

"Next week?" Nora repeated. "The publisher needs it today. Can you get it to me today?"

Not today. Fire me. "I'm sorry, but I've had to go over the paperwork with the lawyer. I'm sure you understand." Maggie was not sure Nora did. "I'm sure the publisher will understand."

"I suggest you spend the weekend getting caught up.

I'll call you Monday. Chop, chop." They disconnected the call.

"What else do I have to do?" Maggie said, opening the manuscript. "It's not like I'm going to be hanging out with Jess this weekend."

Maggie spent the rest of the day working, surprising herself at all the writing she had accomplished. She ordered pizza, watched a movie, and went upstairs to her and Cory's bedroom. After a short crying jag, she crawled into bed. Had Cory and Jess had sex in this bed? She sighed. "I'm definitely moving from here, too."

TWENTY-SIX

NURSE DEBORAH FINISHED giving shift report to the oncoming nurses and walked up to Doctor Bruce, who was writing an order for the drug lorazepam in a patient's chart. The nurses' station was busy as the shift change signaled a change in the day's activity. Patients were waking up and the food cart with breakfast trays was rolling off the elevator.

"Are you finished?" Deborah asked, acting as though they were getting ready to go to a meeting.

He closed the chart and left it lying on the counter. "Yes."

They walked to the elevator and waited for its door to slide open. After a nurse had walked out, they got inside and took it to the basement. They walked past the kitchen, the laundry room, and the storage room, until they came to the last room in the far corner, away from the chatter of busy workers.

"Who's going to be the medium for the séance?" Bruce asked before he opened the door.

"Claudia is doing it because Ethel is at the reception desk."

"I hope the manager isn't joining us, we need to keep this private."

"It's just going to be the three of us."

Bruce opened the door, and they walked into the dark room.

"Claudia's not here yet," Deborah said, walking to the table. She took a lighter from her white skirt pocket and lit three candles on the witchboard tabletop, next to a crystal ball.

Bruce walked up to her and put his hand on a breast. "I could take you right now, baby."

Deborah unbuttoned the top button of his crisp white shirt. "Later, when we're done. We have to take care of business first."

"I see you have the candles lit," Claudia said with her usual high-pitched voice as she walked up behind them. She closed the door, adjusted her shawl, and sat at the table. She pulled the crystal sphere toward her and then motioned for them to sit down. "What would you like me to see?"

Deborah squirmed in her chair and then said, "Well, we need you to put a curse on someone."

Claudia took her hands off the crystal ball. "I do not do curses. Ethel and I only work with spirits from the light." Her eyes narrowed and her voice lowered. "Why do you want to cast a curse?"

Bruce chuckled. "Deborah just misspoke. Curse is too harsh of a word. It would be more like a spell of protection." He looked at Deborah, who was watching him intently, and then back at Claudia. "Do you do that?" Claudia looked away from Bruce and began looking around the room, following something with her eyes. She pulled her shawl even tighter around her shoulders.

"There is a darkness that is being attracted here, to this room, to this place." She stood up and looked at Bruce and Deborah. "I think it is attaching itself to the both of you." She walked toward the door. "It is in your best interest if you leave this room right now. That is what I'm going to do." She paused and looked back at them. "I suggest you both do the same thing and leave this room until it has been cleansed."

Deborah and Bruce watched Claudia leave the room in haste. Deborah got up, closed, and locked the door. They both looked around the room as the candles flickered and cast bouncing shadows on the walls. Even the mirror's frame of intertwining snakes seemed to be coiling about themselves.

"She's making it up," Deborah said, sitting back down. "She just doesn't want us to put a curse on someone. I don't see anything bad in this room and besides, I think we can do it ourselves."

"It won't hurt to try," Bruce said, moving his chair closer to Deborah. "I don't want either one of us being accused of Susan Knight's death. Margaret has to take the fall, not us."

Deborah touched Bruce's hand, and her voice softened, "You know, they say that sexual energy makes curses stronger."

Bruce's hand went to Deborah's breast. "Let's get this spell over with, before I explode."

Deborah moved to Claudia's chair and placed her hands on the crystal ball. "I've never done this before. I don't even know what to say."

"Just say what we need and be done with it."

Deborah caressed the cold globe. "Should I ask for the good spirits or the bad spirits?"

"I don't think good spirits perform curses so you'll have to ask a bad spirit."

"Like who? I don't want the devil showing up."

"Just make something up," Bruce said. "That crystal ball and this room itself must have special powers because Claudia and Ethel keep using it for séances. You should get the spirit we need."

Deborah smiled at Bruce and then turned her attention back toward the sphere in front of her. The light cast from the candles made the ball glow as if it were coming to life. She put her hands gently on it and looked at Bruce. "Put your hands palm down on the table while I begin."

Bruce placed his hands on the witchboard, close to the pentagram carved in the center.

Deborah began. "I summon a spirit who can cast a curse on Margaret McGee." She looked up at Bruce, smiled, and looked back at the crystal. "Is there a spirit who can help us who is in this room right now?"

The candle flames grew in girth and brightness as the room became darker around them.

"I'm feeling an electrical charge from this crystal," Deborah said, excited. "I'm going to say the curse I looked up in a witch's spell book when I went to a bookshop. I don't remember it exactly, but it goes like this." She gazed into the crystal ball. "Power of my will, get me what I want, when I want it, and what I ask. Say what you want, then say bring me my wish and summon evil to do my will so mote it be." Deborah reached into her skirt pocket and took out a driver's license that belonged to Margaret. She sat it on the witchboard, next to the candles. "I will that this Margaret McGee be held responsible for the death of Susan Knight. And that I, Deborah Franklin and

my partner Bruce Hancock, not be held responsible and thus have no negative repercussions from the death."

Bruce cleared his throat. "Summon evil? And where did you get her driver's license?"

Deborah still held her hands to the globe as if glued to it. "I took it from her purse when she was in the bathroom." She continued to look into the globe, her eyes widened. "I see . . . I see something."

"What do you see?"

She smiled. "It's more like I feel something. It's like something is telling me in my head that in order for the curse to be sealed, we need to weaken Margaret's energy."

"How do we do that?"

Goosebumps formed on Deborah's arms. "I'm really getting turned on from this." Her breathing became shallow as she came close to panting. "We need to weaken the white light around her by . . ."

"By what?" Bruce did not take his eyes off Deborah, who was behaving like a real medium.

"We have to give our souls to the evil one and in exchange we will be granted this favor." Her wide eyes were transfixed on the ball as if it had control over her.

"Give our souls to the devil?" Bruce inhaled deeply. "That's a lot to ask. I don't know if that's a good idea."

Debora's eyes rolled up under her upper eyelids as she spoke in a guttural voice that sounded like it belonged to a creature from Hell. "If this curse—the curse that you have begun of your own free will—is not sealed, I will see to it that you live a life of Hell on Earth." Then she screeched. "Seal the curse now!"

Bruce's hands trembled, but he kept them in place on the board. "Okay, I'll do it."

Deborah's eyes returned to normal as she massaged the globe as if she were making love to it. "We accept thy offer and give our souls to thee and vow to seal the curse now." She looked at Bruce as if she was in a trance. "It is done. Everything is fine. All we have to do now is . . ."

Deborah stood and walked to Bruce, who was already unbuckling his pants. While the darkness of the room throbbed to their motions, it intensified the sensations felt, rewarding them for their perfect decision.

TWENTY-SEVEN

MAGGIE WAS NAUSEATED when she awoke with perspiration-soaked linens covering her shivering body that Saturday morning. She ran to the bathroom and dry heaved into the toilet. Her wet nightshirt clung to her chilled body as she knelt on the bath rug, waiting for the sickness to pass.

What is it with these dreams? she said to herself. They are so real as if I am remembering something from the past.

She stood up, went to the sink, and wiped her face with a cold, wet washcloth. She had no energy; it was as if she had been awake all night. Even though she did not feel like taking a shower, she turned the water on, got out of her sticky nightclothes, and showered.

When she had finished and dressed, she walked toward the kitchen to brew coffee, stopping when she caught sight of the dining room table where Cory had been. She took a deep breath and walked through the area to the coffee pot.

She snuck a cup of coffee and walked into the office, sitting in front of her computer. There was no one to talk

to about the dreams. She no longer considered Jess a confidant, or friend for that matter. Maybe she should send an email to Nora about what was going on, but then she reconsidered, not wanting Nora to think she was crazy like everyone else did. On the other hand, she trusted Nora.

Not wanting Nora to get the message immediately and call her with questions before her brain was fully awake, she took a piece of notepaper from the desk drawer and began writing. She told about the dreams, about Jess and the affair with Cory, the missing jewelry, the altered will, and about the crazy people at Sandpiper Bluff and their false accusations. She mentioned that she would leave the apartment when she got the evidence she needed to defend herself. Until then, she would be there with the nutcases who, for some reason, wanted to harm her. She pointed out that the reason she was writing the letter was so that someone she trusted would have a record of her side of the story because she did not trust the people that surrounded her. It seemed as though predators were ruthlessly pursuing her.

She put the letter in a stamped envelope and took it to the mailbox on her way out to the car. She needed to go back to the apartment and check the camcorder. Hopefully, there was something worthwhile on it.

Once again, when Sandpiper Bluff came into view, a feeling of oppression came over her. She became nauseated and wanted to turn the car around; she did not want to be there. Even so, she parked and walked to the building. The sun that was shining brightly when she left her house was now hidden behind dark gray clouds. The wind blew harshly through the trees and no birds were

singing, even the roses refused to release their perfume as if they were afraid to open their petals.

She looked at her empty mailbox and walked inside the gloomy lobby, even the previously shiny staircase banister was dull and in shadow. She looked toward Ethel's apartment, debating whether to speak with her now or later. Even though the old woman believed in the supernatural, she trusted her. She would talk with her tomorrow before she moved out. Yes, tomorrow she was moving out.

As Maggie walked up the stairs, she felt a pressure on her chest as if she was having angina or a myocardial infarction. But the heaviness passed as she reached the second floor. She looked toward Bruce's door as she walked to the apartment, hoping he would not poke his damned head out as he typically did. To her relief, no one confronted her as she unlocked her door and quickly stepped inside. She locked it and looked out the peephole, catching a glimpse of Susie walking up the stairs to the third floor with something in her hand that did not look like the ratty teddy bear she typically held.

Maggie turned away from the door and gasped. There, in the middle of the living room, was Susie's teddy bear. It was sitting up as if someone carefully placed him so he would not fall over.

Her nerves were tingling as if her nervous system had sent out a power surge of electricity to every nerve ending in her body. She stood there listening; hoping whoever had placed the bear for Maggie to find was no longer in the apartment. Other than the wind outside her windows, it was quiet.

Then she looked toward her bedroom to where she had the camcorder hidden. She let out a sigh of relief,

knowing she had caught the perpetrator on camera. She walked into her bedroom and took the camera out from under the blankets. She pressed rewind and sat on the bed to view the recording.

Okay, Debbie, now I got you. She pressed play. She watched for someone to enter the door. Someone did . . . It was her. The camera had only recorded her entering the apartment moments earlier.

The windows, they had to have come in through the windows. With the camera in hand, she went into the living room, past the teddy bear, and tested the windows. They were locked as was every window in the apartment. How could that be? The door was locked, the windows were locked, and there was no other way inside the apartment. The camera did not catch anyone coming in through the door. Was it possible that someone came in the door, found the camera, erased the recording, and then reset it? Yes, that was possible, but the camera would have recorded them leaving through the door, and there was no such recording.

Maggie got the phone from her purse and took a picture of the teddy bear. It would not show the face of the person who came inside her apartment, but it would show that someone had come inside and sat the teddy bear for her to see when she returned.

She put the phone back inside her purse and began to sob. Nothing was working out. Debbie and Bruce were messing with her, and she could not prove it. How could she get proof? If it were not for the accusation of abusing Susie, she would just leave and forget about it. Of course, Susie would know she had not been harmed by Maggie and would stand up for her. Then she thought, Debbie and Bruce probably convinced her to lie, and if

questioned Susie would say that Maggie had abused her. What could she do? The audio recording of Jess was static and the video camera showed no one coming into the apartment except her. She took the skeleton key from her pocket. Yes, she would use it to go inside Debbie and Bruce's apartments. There had to be evidence there.

TWENTY-EIGHT

HOW WOULD SHE know when Debbie and Bruce were not home? All Maggie ever saw were two cars in the parking lot, Ethel's and Mr. Zimmerman's. How were Debbie and Bruce getting around? Were they walking everywhere? Debbie had to be home because she just saw Susie walking upstairs. Maybe she should talk with Ethel and see if she knows what is going on.

Maggie left the teddy bear where it sat, locked the door, and walked down the steps to Ethel's apartment. She knocked. She could hear dishes placed in a sink and then footsteps approach the door. She looked away from the peephole, knowing Ethel must be looking through it. The door opened.

"Hi, dear; come in." Ethel swung the door wide-open and closed it behind Maggie. "I've

CONNIE MYRES

been expecting you. Please have a seat." Ethel pointed to a small table draped with a paisley cloth in the middle of the room.

Maggie mimicked Ethel and sat in one of the small chairs. She smiled, the atmosphere inside Ethel's apartment was light, even though the sky outside was darkening. The air smelled of pungent incense or

marijuana. "What incense are you using? It smells like . . . pot."

Ethel lit a single candle on the table and laughed. "It's not pot; it is sage. I was burning it because it cleanses spaces and people."

"Oh, sorry." Maggie watched as Ethel got up and closed the curtains, darkening the room. Colored beads hung over a doorway, and a lamp in the corner had a colorful cloth draped over the shade, casting a cheerful reddish glow into the room. "I'm getting the feeling you knew I was coming."

Ethel leaned toward Maggie. "I thought it was likely, and I'm glad you did. Do you mind if I read you?"

"No, not at all; I wanted to talk to you; I have a couple questions."

"Hold out your hand, I'd like to begin by reading, or rather, feeling your palm."

Maggie put her hand, palm up, on the table in front of Ethel.

"I'm a seer, so you may notice me closing my eyes and making strange movements while I go into a trance." She adjusted the green scarf tied like a headband and looked at Maggie. "In other words, don't be alarmed. Since I don't use a crystal ball anymore, I have to improvise."

"There's a crystal ball in the basement."

Ethel reached for Maggie's hand and held it firmly in hers. "What? Don't tell me you've been inside that room?"

Maggie shrugged. "When I was doing laundry, the door was open and Bruce showed me around."

Ethel's grip tightened. "That door is locked. It has been locked since a demon entered that room back in

1969." Ethel shook her head. "Things may be worse than I expected. Don't ever go back in that room again."

"Okay," Maggie said, surprised by Ethel's reaction.

Ethel relaxed her shoulders and closed her eyes, still holding Maggie's hand. She slowed her breathing and was silent for several minutes, and then said, "Maggie, you have the white light of protection around you. It is a gift that has been passed down from your ancestors. You have a good soul, but good souls are like honey to flies; attracting nasty creatures that thrive on sucking the life from them and using it to strengthen themselves."

Maggie watched as Ethel's smile disappeared, replaced by tight, over-lipsticked lips.

"You have a dark entity attached to you. It has been there for decades, even before you were born. It was put there by people with dirty souls . . . Souls who no longer have human bodies. Souls condemned to roam the earth, never to be reincarnated or to live again. They are dead forever, having sold their souls to the devil in exchange for a greedy favor."

Maggie cleared her throat. "I don't know what you mean."

Ethel's frowning eyes stayed closed. "It's becoming clearer. The demon that has been in this building has grown since you moved in. The demon is fueling two lost souls." Ethel groaned as if in pain. "Souls that you encountered decades ago . . . souls that keep reaffirming their commitment to Satan, who gives them pleasures . . . pleasures stronger than any earthly pleasure ever could be . . . their perfect Hell on Earth."

Maggie watched tears form around Ethel's tightly closed eyes. "Are you okay, Ethel?"

"It's you the entity wants . . . It needs your soul to fuel it. It took it before, but you were able to break away. Unknown to you, it summoned you here, to the place where it all began. It is trying to steal your soul and feed upon it."

Maggie felt compelled to ask her question. "Debbie and Bruce are telling lies about me, are they part of it?"

Ethel looked like she was shaking something off her head as she gripped Maggie's hand, preventing her from leaving the table. "Who are Debbie and Bruce?"

"You know, the people who live on the second floor with the little girl, Susie."

Ethel sobbed. Tears streamed down her cheeks, dripped off her chin and onto her gypsy skirt. "Maggie, there is no one on the second floor, only you."

Maggie could not speak. Of course there were people on the second floor. "But . . . there are people. I've talked to them and even babysat Susie."

Ethel's head dropped forward. "I see it clearly, Maggie. You once worked here as a nurse on the second floor when this place was used as a psychiatric hospital. The Debbie and Bruce you talk about must be the two souls condemned to Hell, and you are the victim.

In 1969, there was a little girl named Susan Knight, who was admitted to the hospital. She was a raging mess when they brought her in here; acting as though she was possessed by a demon. Anyway, she was accidentally killed while a patient on the second floor. You were blamed for the death because of the deal the two people made with the devil. I believe their names were Deborah Franklin and Dr. Bruce Hancock. There were rumors about them being the guilty ones, not you. But something happened, somehow you died . . . And they died, too. You

were brought back to live again, but the two condemned souls still want revenge for not being allowed to live the rest of their human lives in the bliss promised to them. They want you to suffer."

Maggie could not believe what she was hearing. "But they're there; I'll prove it to you."

Ethel opened her red eyes and looked at Maggie. "You must leave this place now before it's too late," she let go of Maggie's hand. "I fear it is already too late."

Maggie's hand tingled as she rubbed it with her other hand. Ethel was speaking craziness. "Come upstairs with me and I'll prove it to you. There are other renters on the floor."

Ethel shook her head as she reached for a wood tip cigar.

"Please, Ethel." Maggie had to prove to herself, even more than Ethel, that she had not been talking to ghosts all this time.

Ethel stood and took a delicately embroidered handkerchief from a coin purse sitting on an end table beside a dusty wing chair and dabbed at her eyes. "If I go with you, and you find no one on the second floor, will you leave that instant?"

"If I find there are no people on the second floor I'll probably check myself into a mental hospital," Maggie half-heartedly smiled.

"You didn't answer my question." "Yes, I'll leave. No doubt about it."

TWENTY-NINE

"ARE YOU READY to check the apartments on the second floor?" Ethel asked, giving her wet eyes one last dab.

"I am, let's go," Maggie said, walking toward the door.

They walked out of Ethel's first floor apartment and past Mr. Zimmerman's office toward the staircase.

Maggie stopped on the first step and looked back at Ethel, who was still holding the thin cigar in her hand. "So, you're saying that only you and Mr. Zimmerman live here?"

Ethel took a short drag on the thin brown cigar and then blew the white smoke toward the floor. "That's right. No one has lived on the second floor since it was renovated into apartments several years ago. I'm surprised Mr. Zimmerman let you rent an apartment there.

He must be desperate for rent money; the place does need a lot of repairs."

Maggie put her hand on the handrail gummed with dirt from years of use. She looked at the rail and removed her hand. Every time she looked at the stairway, it seemed

older than when she first arrived. "Is it possible people are squatting in those apartments?"

Ethel shook her head. "I would have seen them. There have been no signs of anyone else in the building for years." Ethel let ashes fall to the floor. "Think about the names, Maggie. You said they called themselves Debbie, Bruce, and Susie. Those are the names from the past; even your name. The four of you are tied together, and the link needs to be broken."

Maggie turned and began walking up the staircase.

When she got to the top, Ethel stood beside her.

"I'll check Debbie's apartment first." Maggie walked up to apartment 21B and knocked on the door. There was no answer, so she knocked again, still no answer.

Ethel looked at Maggie with raised eyebrows and a look of, *I told you so*.

"I'll try Bruce's." Maggie walked to his door and knocked. Just as no one answered at Debbie's, no one answered at Bruce's. She reached into her pocket, took out her key ring, and held up the skeleton key for Ethel to see. "It should open their doors."

Ethel choked and coughed. "Where'd you get that?" "Mr. Zimmerman gave it to me. Does your apartment

use one?"

"No, my apartment does not use one. I knew the developer stopped renovating when the workers refused to come back because they were afraid. I heard that their tools were being moved, they would see apparitions, and one worker even was pushed down the stairway by unseen hands. I guess the locks were one thing they never got to, but Mr. Zimmerman should have replaced them. Especially since there were renters up here for a couple years, but they quickly left, just like the workers." Ethel

looked toward the French doors as rain began to pelt the glass. "When I worked as a receptionist here, decades ago, I would see the nurses with those passkeys."

"Mr. Zimmerman is a cheapskate because my bed is an old hospital bed."

Ethel's hand quivered as she put the cigar in her mouth, letting it hang from the corner of her wrinkled lips. "When you see no one is here, I'm helping you pack and you're moving into my apartment until you find someplace else."

That Saturday afternoon turned dark from the storm, making it seem as though it was the middle of the night. The rain smacking into the porch doors caused them to rattle as Maggie put the skeleton key into Bruce's door and unlocked it. She turned the doorknob and opened it.

Flashes of lightning through the windows revealed an abandoned apartment. Not abandoned by Bruce, but by a renter who left without clearing the table or even bothering to take all of their belongings with them. The Formica table and the turquoise vinyl chairs were the same she had sat in when Bruce invited her to supper, except dust covered the seats. The table had the rose porcelain teapot and three teacups, one of which looked recently used. By her? Had she sleepwalked and dreamed she had tea with Bruce?

"See, Maggie, no one lives here," Ethel said, standing at the door.

"It was so real. I've been in here because that's the cup I drank from; it had chamomile tea and honey."

Ethel saw the recently used cup.

"Maggie, I fear that you've stepped through a veil into the spirit world," Ethel said, backing up. "Please close the door."

Maggie pulled the door shut and walked to Debbie's apartment. Her hands fumbled turning the key in the lock. She knew this apartment would be empty, too. She opened the door, and as a bright flash of lightning filled the room, she saw Debbie and Bruce standing side-by-side, looking at her. Thunder instantly cracked, causing the electricity to go out. But as the lightning flashed like strobe lights, she saw them raise their arms toward her, summoning her to enter.

Ethel pulled Maggie backward and closed the door. "Let's get your things, now, and get out of here."

Maggie was shocked and confused as Ethel took the key from Maggie's hand, went to her apartment, and opened the door. "Do you have a flashlight?" She looked at Maggie whose brain was still digesting the events. She shook Maggie's shoulders. "Maggie, snap out of it. We need light."

Ethel's touch brought Maggie back. She reached into her purse and took out her phone to use as a light, but it would not power on. "The batteries must be dead."

"Get your computer and anything important that you can carry and let's get out of here. You're never coming back to this room." Ethel stepped into the apartment while the air alternated between flashes of light and pitch-blackness. She walked forward, tripped, and fell. She moaned.

Maggie went up to her. "Are you all right?"

Ethel held her hip as Susie's teddy bear sat solemnly on the floor looking at them. "I tripped on that damned bear, and I hurt my hip."

"Is it broken?"

Ethel wiggled her toes and then raised a knee. "I don't think so, but I'm not going to be able to walk so well."

"Stay there," Maggie said, going to the kitchen. She put her laptop and camera into her backpack and then rushed about the apartment filling it to overflowing. She put her purse cross-body and then put the pack on her back before kicking the bear into a corner and kneeling down next to Ethel. "I'll help you up."

Ethel groaned in pain as she limped to the door with Maggie acting as a crutch. When they walked out of the apartment, the power flickered back on. "We'll have to take the elevator because I can't walk down the steps."

Maggie did not want to go into that contraption, but she was not strong enough to carry Ethel. "What if the power goes out while we're in there?"

"You're right, let's take the stairs."

Then the elevator door opened, waiting for them to enter.

"I'm still not going in there," Maggie said, helping Ethel to the stairs.

"Someone's coming up the stairs," Ethel said, looking toward the first floor lobby.

"You see her?" Maggie was relieved that Ethel could see what she was seeing. Unfortunately, what Maggie was seeing was Susie walking one slow jittery step at a time toward them.

"We have to get to my apartment where it's safe," Ethel said as they stood there watching Susie get closer. "Can we walk past her?"

Another surge of adrenaline shot through Maggie's body. "No, she has a knife."

THIRTY

"LET'S GO BACK in my apartment," Maggie said, helping Ethel turn. But there was no going back, Debbie and Bruce were blocking the entry. "I guess the elevator is our only way out of here."

Ethel's cigar—which she held clenched in her teeth—fell to the dirty floor as they tried to make it to the elevator before the spirits reached them.

They went inside the ancient elevator, and Maggie began frantically pressing the first floor button. The door was not closing. Susie was coming into view . . . Susie and the knife . . . Susie and the bloody knife. The child's head faced the floor as stringy hair covered her face.

"Come on, come on, come on," Maggie said, repeatedly pressing the button as Susie reached the second floor and turned toward them.

Ethel reached up and touched the side of Maggie's face. "Calm down and think. Think of surrounding us with white light, child. Close your eyes and feel it."

Maggie was about to scream before Ethel touched her face. She felt a calmness fill her as she closed her eyes and

did as Ethel said. The elevator doors closed; she opened her eyes. They were descending.

The lights in the cab blinked on and off. Maggie looked at Ethel who appeared to have put herself into a trance. She looked back toward the door as the elevator stopped. If the doors opened in the basement, she would have to die and put an end to this misery because she could not take it any longer.

As the door screeched open, Maggie saw Mr. Zimmerman's office—still vacant of the superintendent. They were on the first floor. "Ethel, time to go."

"No, not to your car," Ethel said, resisting Maggie's efforts to leave the building. "They'll follow us. We need to go to my apartment where it is safe, and we'll be protected."

Maggie let out a deep breath and looked toward the stairway; Susie was on her way down. "You better be right because they could hack through your door or break your windows to get in."

Ethel winced as Maggie pulled her faster than she wanted to go. "They're spirits, Maggie, not live humans."

When they reached Ethel's apartment, they went inside and locked the door. Maggie helped Ethel to the couch, gently putting her legs up and a pillow under her head.

"Maggie, bring me that tin box," Ethel said, pointing toward a shiny golden box on a shelf.

Maggie brought the box to her. She watched as Ethel took out a canister and handed it to her. "I've already done this, but take this blessed salt and pour it at the base of the door and the windows; it will keep them from getting in."

She did as Ethel instructed, first pouring a thin line in front of the door. Then she went to the windows, moved the closed curtains aside, and poured some along the windowsill. She looked out into the storm, seeing nothing but torrential rain and lightning, no spirits. When she finished, she went back to Ethel. "It's done."

Ethel grimaced as she changed positions on the sofa. "We'll be fine. Soon they'll go back where they came from."

Maggie watched as Ethel rubbed her right hip. "I think you should go to the emergency room and get an x-ray; it could be broken."

"It's fine," she said, disregarding Maggie's suggestion. "It's just my arthritis. Whenever a joint gets moved more than it should, my arthritis kicks in and causes trouble." She pulled herself up to a half-sitting position. "Speaking of trouble, I could use the oxycodone in my kitchen cabinet by the sink. It's sitting next to a bottle of bourbon—bring them both, will ya, dear?"

Maggie put her hands on her hips. "I'll get them for you but you know you're not supposed to take a narcotic with alcohol."

Ethel smiled. "I'm in severe pain. I just need something to ease it and help me relax."

Maggie returned with the pill bottle, a glass of water, and the bourbon whiskey, sitting them on the end table next to the couch. She watched as Ethel took a pill and washed it down with water. "Thank you for not drinking the whiskey."

Ethel leaned back as the apartment lights flickered. "The bourbon is my backup."

"Should I call the police?" Maggie asked, keeping her eyes on the door.

"The police for what; to report ghosts are chasing you? They won't believe you and besides, there's nothing they could do anyway."

Maggie walked to the wall phone. "We should check on Mr. Zimmerman and make sure he's okay."

"The number's right there by the phone."

Maggie dialed Mr. Zimmerman, but as usual, there was no answer. "When is the last time you saw Mr. Zimmerman?"

Ethel took the bottle of bourbon into her hand. "It's been a couple days . . . maybe a few days, but I don't see him that often, anyway."

"Could those spirits harm him?" Maggie sat in the dusty wing chair. "Susie had a knife, and she went to the third floor."

Ethel opened the bottle and took a swig of the biting liquid. "Maybe."

"I need to check on him," Maggie said, leaning forward with elbows on her knees. "I haven't seen him since the first day I moved in."

Ethel took one more swig and repositioned her pillow. "It's not safe for you, or I, to go back out there. We'll check on Mr. Zimmerman in the morning. I'm sure he's fine . . . At least I hope so."

THIRTY-ONE

MAGGIE WALKED INTO Ethel's spare room. It smelled of mothballs and burnt sage. She wanted to plug her cell phone into an outlet, but she had left the charger in her apartment during the rush to get out; she would go to her apartment in the morning and retrieve it. Until then, she would crawl into bed and forget about the day while Ethel slept on the couch.

She lay in bed, looking around the dark room. The thick walls of the old building dulled the sound of thunder, but not enough for her to forget there was a storm outside. She considered the possibility of spirits reaching through the walls, grabbing her, and carrying her to Hell with them.

Maggie left her bedroom door open, wanting some connection with Ethel, who seemed to know how to keep them safe. She could hear Ethel set a bottle on the end table. She must have swallowed more whiskey, Maggie thought as she turned on her side and closed her eyes.

🜋 🜋 🜋

MAGGIE STOOD ON a dock next to a thirty-six-foot mahogany cruiser. On the deck was Debbie, dressed in a pink and white string bikini and big sunglasses. Maggie quickly looked at her clothes, hoping she was not dressed the same way. She was relieved to see sandals on her feet, and shorts and a blouse covering the rest of her body.

"Are you coming or not?" Debbie asked. She was so giddy that she fell into Bruce, who had walked up next to her.

Maggie heard waves lap against the hull and their hollow swish underneath the dock. She felt a warm breeze against her hot skin. It must be close to ninety degrees, she thought. When she looked at Bruce, he was smiling at her. His belted green and black striped swim trunks suddenly made her realize she was back in time and looking at Dr. Bruce Hancock and Deborah, the nurse.

Bruce held out a hand. "I'll help you; I won't let you fall."

Maggie did not want to get on the boat. Nothing good was going to come from being around Bruce and Deborah. She began turning around and was about to walk away when Bruce reached for her and pulled her into the boat.

"We're all aboard," Bruce shouted toward the helm. He held her close to his body before releasing her and untying the boat from the dock's cleats.

Maggie reassured herself that this was only a dream and that she would wake up in Ethel's apartment soon. When she turned around, she saw a man at the helm. He looked like the man in the photograph in Mr. Zimmerman's office. This had to be Mr. Zimmerman's

father. He gave the boat's horn one blast and then left the dock, pulling into the fairway toward Lake Michigan.

"Are you seasick, Margaret?" Deborah asked, leaning against the guardrail. Then she picked up a nautical beach towel and made her way to the foredeck before Maggie had a chance to answer.

Maggie watched Bruce follow Deborah to the bow, like a dog in heat. However, she decided to stay where she was; she did not want to get close to the people who—according to a previous flashback—wanted to blame her for Susan's death. What was the point of this dream? She held her hair, keeping it from turning into a tangled mess, as the captain left the channel and headed toward the open water. The boat bounced and waves splashed until they reached an area far from the shoreline. The captain turned off the engine and approached Maggie with a bottle of Scotch in his hand and some plastic cups. Maggie stared at the bottle of brown liquid. All she could think of was Claudia's words when she had first met her at Lenny's Grocery. *My daddy once said Carl killed a man out there on the water, right there in front of Lake*

Shore Sanatorium—all liquored up on Scotch, he was.

He handed her a cup with a couple shots. "Here you go, ma'am."

Maggie took the cup from him, and then asked, "Is your name Carl?"

He smiled and tipped his white sailor cap. "Captain Carl Zimmerman, at your service."

Maggie imagined she looked as white as a ghost, but she was not a ghost; he was the ghost. He was someone from the past, someone who killed a man.

"You don't have sea legs, do you, ma'am?" he said.

Maggie's mouth was dry. "It's just that you look familiar. Do you have any children?"

"I have one son, Carl Jr. He works as a janitor at that god-awful place they call a hospital." He poured himself a shot of Scotch into a cup, swallowed it, and pointed toward the distant shore. "That's the place right there. They call it Lake Shore Sanatorium and Psychiatric Hospital." He leaned so close to her that she could smell the liquor on his breath. He whispered, "I think the people who work there should be patients. They're all off their rockers. I heard that if there is one more incident, they're going to shut that place down, and people are going to pay. Some will lose their professional licenses and others will get jail time; serves them bastards' right for treating innocent people like dogs."

Maggie nodded. "Yeah, it's not a very nice place." "Sorry, I don't want to ruin your weekend." He took a

handkerchief from his fishing vest, blew his nose, and stuffed it back into one of the vest's many pockets.

"Oh, you're not," Maggie said, but she knew this trip was not going to end well.

"I'm going up with the others; you should join us." He turned and walked to the bow and sat across from Bruce and Deborah.

Maggie looked across the blue water toward shore. There, on the bluff, was the sanatorium. It looked majestic, like a mansion for a wealthy lumber baron. At the same time, it was eerie looking.

"Hey, Margaret," Deborah said. "Why don't you come up here and join us."

It's only a dream. It's only a dream; she kept reminding herself as she stood up and walked to the head

of the boat. When she passed the cabin, she smelled a foul odor. "Is there a dead animal on board?"

"That's just the leftover smell of a propane leak from the stove that I had earlier. It's fixed; there's nothing to worry about," the captain said.

Maggie was not sure there was nothing to worry about. Captain Zimmerman must have been drunk before they undocked, and she did not trust his judgment. Nonetheless, the four of them sat talking, laughing, and drinking for a couple hours.

When Bruce returned from the bathroom, he had Deborah's beach bag in his hand. He sat it next to her and put his hand on her bare thigh.

"Time to check your blood sugar, babe," Bruce said. "Don't want to forget that." Deborah giggled as she

reached into the bag and took out a small case with a glucose meter inside. She poked her finger, drawing a drop of blood, which she then placed on a strip in the machine. "It's fine, eighty-eight."

Maggie noticed the captain squirm in his seat and then tense up as if he had seen something frightening. Then she saw Bruce sneer at the captain.

"Margaret, let me test your blood sugar," Deborah said, approaching Maggie with the lancet.

"I'm not diabetic, I don't need it checked."

"You know how alcohol can cause hypoglycemia." Deborah kneeled next to Maggie and reached for her hand.

"Don't let her touch you," the captain said. He reached over and pushed Deborah's hand away. "They're not what they seem."

As far as Maggie was concerned, nobody was as they seemed; not even herself. She braced herself on the seat as

the water became choppy and dark clouds began approaching the boat. "What's going on?"

The captain pointed between Bruce and Deborah. "There's a hooded . . . something in a black hooded robe." "You're drunk, old man," Deborah said. She reached

for Maggie's hand and punctured the skin on a fingertip with the lancet.

Maggie jumped from the poke, but Deborah held her hand tight as blood dripped into a small glass ampoule.

"What are you doing?" Maggie tugged her hand away. "That's not a test strip."

Deborah returned to Bruce, put the capped tube into the meter's case, and returned it to her bag. Then both Bruce and Deborah looked at the terrified captain.

"Do you see it, Margaret?" Captain Zimmerman asked, reaching inside his vest as if he was having a heart attack.

Maggie shook her head and held her sore finger as cold raindrops began to fall from the black swirling sky above.

Bruce looked at Deborah. "Who would've thought a drunken sailor could see our friend."

They laughed. Then, without warning, Bruce stood and lunged for the captain. Maggie began screaming as Bruce tried to push the captain overboard.

Then a single gunshot broke through the wind with a crack. Bruce stumbled backward, falling at Deborah's feet. Deborah sprang at the captain and began clawing at his face, causing him to drop the snub-nosed revolver he had hidden under his garment before she managed to push him over the side of the boat.

Maggie reached down and picked up the gun while Deborah watched a massive swell pull the captain under.

"You bitch," Deborah said as she returned to Bruce and knelt next to him. He was lying face down and groaning in pain. Blood rushed from underneath him as the rain diluted and washed it down the deck.

Maggie stood when Deborah stood. She pointed the gun at Deborah. "Stay away or I'll shoot."

Deborah smiled, rolled her eyes, and raised her hands. "Are you going to kill an innocent person like you did Susan?"

"I didn't kill Susan, you did."

"No, not true." Deborah began taking small steps toward Maggie. "It's already in the record what happened. Now . . ." Deborah pointed toward Bruce, "you've killed Bruce and the captain. You're sick Margaret."

Maggie shook her head and began backing toward the cabin, trying to stay a few feet ahead of Deborah.

"Where're you going, Maggie? All that's left is overboard like the captain."

Maggie knew there had to be a marine radio at the helm, so she kept backing her way toward it, while Deborah kept following her.

"You're a pitiful case, Margaret McGee. Maybe they'll give you the death penalty and put you out of your misery."

Gusts of wind rocked the boat as Maggie turned and ran to the helm. She picked up the radio's handset, pressed the button on the side, and frantically said, "Mayday! Mayday! Mayday!"

It was no use. Deborah ran up to her and began clawing at Maggie's face, causing her to drop the handset and stumble backward into the lower-level galley. While lying on the floor, next to the stove, she could smell the

propane—it was still leaking. Deborah was on top of Maggie, trying to take the gun from her hands.

Maggie whispered, "It's only a dream. It's only a dream." She squeezed the trigger, knowing it would spark and cause the propane to explode. In the slow-motion seconds before the explosion, she knew she would die. Then, she thought, hadn't she already died?

THIRTY-TWO

AS MAGGIE TRANSITIONED from sleep to wakefulness, she crossed her arms and felt her damp skin. She did not remember feeling any pain when the boat in her dream exploded. It was as if her soul had left the body before the rapid combustion scattered pieces of flesh and bone over the agitated water.

She sat up. Night sweats had soaked her shirt with perspiration. Anxiety from the flashback, she thought. Fortunately, she had stuffed another shirt and pair of underpants into her backpack before leaving her apartment yesterday. However, she still needed her phone charger. After she showered, she would go up to her apartment, get it, and then leave this place, for the last time.

When Maggie had finished showering, she walked into the living room. Ethel was still snoring on the couch. A thin line of drool ran from her mouth, down her cheek, and onto the pillow.

"Ethel, are you awake?" Maggie wanted to let her know that she was going up to her apartment, but Ethel was out. Too much booze and pills, she thought. She

would come back down when she finished and leave a note for Ethel if she were still not awake.

Maggie held her apartment key in her hand as she walked out of Ethel's door. The storm had passed, and the sun was shining; there were no signs of Bruce, Debbie, or Susie. She closed the door and walked to Mr. Zimmerman's office; he was not there. I should speak with him before I leave, she thought.

She looked toward the staircase. Was it safe to climb? She tiptoed toward it. Maybe she should wait for Ethel to wake up and have her go with her to get the rest of her belongings. However, she knew Ethel would not go with her because she did not want her to go back into the apartment. Maggie kept walking toward the stairs, looking up at the second floor and listening. There were no sounds of people, or spirits, moving around; only the sound of occasional clicks and taps in the walls.

The summer sun cast warm rays into the building, making her think that it had the capability of repelling evil. Just as fictional vampires exposed to sunlight will spontaneously combust, maybe these spirits would react the same way. Had she seen them in the sunlight? They were always inside the building. Then she thought, there is no such thing as vampires, and even if there were, these lost souls were not vampires.

Maggie reached the top step on the second floor and looked over at her apartment door; it was closed. She looked up the next flight of stairs leading to the third floor and Mr. Zimmerman's apartment. Maybe she should speak with him first, tell him she was moving out, and then come down and get the rest of her things.

She walked around to the third flight and looked toward the top. She had never been on the third floor.

One light foot at a time, she climbed the stairs. If it were not for the sound of the soles of her shoes grinding dirt into the wood steps, there was no sound. She felt alone in the building. All alone and frightened.

When she reached the top floor, she noticed a sign next to an apartment door with the superintendent's name on it. That must be Mr. Zimmerman's apartment.

She walked across the hall and knocked gently on the door, not wanting to draw attention to the fact she was upstairs.

There was no answer. She knocked again, this time a little louder. Still no answer. Where was Mr. Zimmerman? He has not been answering his phone or in his office. Maybe he was hurt or sick and needed help, she thought, as she turned his doorknob. The door opened.

"Mr. Zimmerman, it's Maggie," she said from the doorway. "Are you home?"

There was no answer. She would need to go inside and check on him. Maybe he had a stroke or a heart attack and was lying ill on the floor. She walked inside the L-shaped living room. His apartment was larger than hers was, she thought as she called his name again.

The living room had magazines stacked on the floor next to a recliner and smelled of rotten meat. A TV tray with a half-eaten plate of food sat next to it. When she walked closer, she noticed flies on the food and the stench of something more rotten than a TV dinner.

Her heart pounded rapidly; she knew something was wrong because the bit of food on the plate could not cause the gagging odor filling his apartment. She forced herself to look around the corner of the room toward the bedroom. The door was open. She kept her hands over her nose as she walked closer. When she looked inside,

she screamed. Mr. Zimmerman was lying face down with all four limbs tied taut to the legs of his bed. Whoever did this to the poor man did not stop there; they had taken something sharp and stabbed his back repeatedly.

Maggie was shaking as she searched for Mr. Zimmerman's phone. Finding a wall phone by the kitchen, she picked it up and dialed 9-1-

1. As she spoke with the dispatcher, she heard someone climbing the stairs.

"I hear someone," she whispered, looking toward the open apartment door.

THIRTY-THREE

SHE DROPPED THE phone, leaving the receiver dangling by its coiled cord, and ran to the door. She was about to close it when she noticed that it was Ethel, limping up the steps like a resurrected mummy pursuing the archaeologists who disturbed his tomb.

"Ethel, thank god," Maggie said, running up to her. "I'm talking to nine-one-one, you stay here, and I'll be right back."

Maggie went back into the apartment, picked up the phone, and continued speaking to the dispatcher. She hung up as Ethel walked inside.

"Is Mr. Zimmerman . . . dead?" Ethel took the scarf from around her head and used it to cover her nose.

Maggie nodded. "We're supposed to leave his apartment so that we don't contaminate anything. I'll open the front door when the police get here."

Maggie helped Ethel set down on the top step. "Did you see Mr. Zimmerman?"

Maggie nodded and looked at the floor. She did not want to talk about it.

"Did he have a coronary . . . or was it something else?"

"Something else."

Ethel took a cigar from her pocket and lit it.

"I don't know if you should smoke that, it might contaminate the area."

"It'll mask the smell and besides, I'm too sore to walk back down the steps."

Maggie agreed and walked down the hallway to a window where she would see the police driving down the driveway. They waited in silence, occasionally giving each other a reassuring smile.

"They're here. I'll be right back," Maggie said, walking past Ethel and down the staircase. She let the officers in and took them up to Mr. Zimmerman's apartment.

After an officer had instructed Ethel to stop smoking, he wrote down Maggie and Ethel's names and addresses while another police officer set up a boundary with yellow crime scene tape and orange cones. He questioned both of them about their accounts of the incident as a man with a tie came up the stairs. When he got closer, Maggie noticed he had a police badge on the left breast and a firearm clipped to the belt of dark gray dress slacks.

"Hi, Detective Becker," the officer said, turning his attention from Maggie and Ethel to the detective.

Detective Becker stepped past Ethel, still sitting on the top step, and smiled at Maggie as he walked into the crime scene with the officer.

Ethel looked up at Maggie and grinned. "He's a crime scene investigator, like on TV . . . and he likes you."

"Shush, not so loud," Maggie said, blushing. "They'll hear you."

Ethel groaned as she changed position. "Are they done with us yet? My butt is getting sore."

Maggie listened to the conversations in Mr. Zimmerman's apartment. She heard someone mention that the weapon that inflicted the fatal wounds had not been found. And that, even though, the victim had been dead for a few days, there appeared to be recent stab wounds, as well. It was Susie, Maggie thought. She had a knife and had gone to the third floor. But Susie was a ghost. Can a ghost use a real knife and kill someone?

The detective took his gloves off, disposed of them, and walked out of the apartment and up to Maggie. "Hi, I'm Detective John Becker, the crime scene investigator. Are you Margaret McGee?"

She nodded. "Yes, I'm Maggie."

"Do you mind if I ask you a few questions?"

"No, not at all," Maggie said, looking at the handsome detective. He was about her age and seemed to have a gentle demeanor by the way he carried himself with calm self-assurance.

"Officer Kline already briefed me on your answers to his questions, but I was wondering how many times you have been here, at Mr. Zimmerman's apartment."

"This is the first time. I moved in only a couple of weeks ago."

"Your apartment is 22C on the second floor, correct?" "Yes, that's right."

"Have you seen anyone come up to this floor?"

"I saw Susie . . ." She stopped speaking mid-sentence. Susie was a spirit from the past. Then movement caught her attention over the detective's right shoulder. Debbie and Bruce were standing several feet behind him. She stared at them as they laughed at her.

"Who is Susie?" the detective asked.

Maggie could not take her eyes off the two of them. "She's ah . . ."

Ethel grunted as she stood up, moved toward Maggie, and stood next to her.

Detective Becker watched Maggie's eyes. "What are you looking at?"

Maggie pointed past the detective. "Do you see them?"

He turned around. "See who?"

"Debbie and Bruce; they live on the second floor." Maggie looked back at the detective, knowing he was beginning to doubt her integrity. "I mean, they used to live there."

"Are you seeing them now?" He kept glancing at Maggie and the hall behind him.

She shook her head even though she was still looking at them. "I'm sorry; I haven't had much sleep lately. My husband committed suicide several weeks ago, and I guess I'm just not back to myself."

"When was the last time Susie came here?" he asked. His voice was not as soft as when he had first begun speaking with her.

"Yesterday . . . No, I don't know." Maggie knew she was beginning to sound crazy.

"You're a guilty, stupid bitch," Debbie said as Bruce pulled her closer. Then she spoke louder, "Detective, Detective, Maggie killed Mr. Zimmerman."

"No, I didn't," Maggie snapped. "Stop accusing me."

Detective Becker looked surprised. "Who's accusing you?"

Maggie shook her head and began to cry.

"She needs rest," Ethel said, touching Maggie's arm. "She's been through a lot."

"How long have you known Maggie?" Detective Becker asked.

Ethel looked at the floor then up at the detective. "Only a couple weeks but we've become good friends."

"Have you seen anyone come up here?"
"No, no I haven't."

"Have you seen anyone else on the second floor?"

She shook her head. "No. The only other person I've seen in the building is her friend, and that was a week ago."

Bruce walked up directly behind Detective Becker and began speaking next to his ear. "Maggie killed him. Maggie killed him. Maggie killed him."

"Don't listen to him, he's lying to you," Maggie said as tears rolled down her face. She looked away from Bruce's fiendish glare.

"Who's lying to me?"

"Bruce." Maggie sobbed. "Bruce and Debbie are lying."

As the officers took bags of evidence from the apartment, the first responding officer came out and stood next to the detective. "Do you need me to make a call?"

The detective looked back at Maggie. "Ma'am, would you like me to call a counselor for you?"

Maggie did not answer as she watched Bruce and Debbie continue to talk as if the detective could hear every word they were saying. Maybe his subconscious could, she thought. If that was the case, she was doomed.

"She'll be fine. She can stay with me." Ethel said, pulling on Maggie's hand. "Dear, come with me . . . if

you're done questioning us, Detective." She looked at the detective with sweet old lady eyes.

Detective Becker gave them both his business card. "I'll be back in touch with both of you soon. Call me if you think of anything regarding this case."

Ethel took the cards. "Thank you, Detective, we will.

Come along, Maggie."

The detective and the officer watched as Ethel, limping from her sore hip, guided Maggie to the elevator. "We need to keep an eye on them," the officer said,

crossing his arms.

"I agree." Detective Becker did not stop watching them until the elevator door closed.

THIRTY-FOUR

ETHEL NOTICED MAGGIE had pushed the second floor button. "Maggie, you're going with me to my apartment, not yours."

She sniffed and wiped her nose with the back of her hand. "I need to get my phone charger. I won't be long."

The elevator bounced to a stop on the second floor. Then, when the cab decided it was ready, the door rumbled open. Maggie and Ethel stepped out.

"I'll be right back." Maggie walked across the hall to her apartment, avoiding the temptation to look at Bruce and Debbie's doors. When she got to hers, she noticed it was unlocked. Not surprising because of the speed at which her and Ethel had left the apartment yesterday.

Maggie left the door open and walked inside while Ethel stood in the hall. She went into her bedroom and unplugged the phone charger from the wall. She looked around. There were still lots of things she wanted to take with her, so she opened her big rolling suitcase and began taking the remaining clothes from the closet and dresser draws. Then she went to the bathroom and began collecting things that would not fit into her backpack

yesterday. She pushed the shower curtain aside and took the wet shampoo and conditioner bottles out. She would need to dry them off before putting them into her suitcase. I will just put them in the laundry basket, she thought as she walked out of the bathroom.

The basket was still sitting next to the bathroom door. When she dropped the bottles onto the dirty towels, she heard a dull clunk, there was something hard underneath them. However, nothing hard should be in the laundry basket. For a moment, she thought it was her video camera, but she had taken it yesterday, and besides, she never hid it in the laundry basket.

Maggie bent over and slowly pushed a towel and the bottles to the side. She screamed. Not an ordinary scream of *help me*, but a cry of anguish; of *I cannot take this anymore*. She backed up to the wall and began hyperventilating.

Detective Becker ran into the room while Ethel waited outside. He followed Maggie's eyes to the laundry basket. There, once hidden in the pile of dirty laundry, was a bloody knife. He put gloves on and inspected the curved blade, stained with blood.

"Is this yours, Ms. McGee?" He looked at her with suspicion.

Maggie stopped screaming, but she was still shaking uncontrollably. She could not stop the movements or even speak.

Two other police officers came into the room with hands resting on their sidearms.

"I think we found the weapon. It's a karambit and is designed for slashing." The detective stood and looked at Maggie. He asked again, "Is this knife yours?"

Maggie shook her head. "No, I've never seen it before." Movement behind the detective caught her attention; it was Bruce and Debbie. "Go away, leave me alone."

"Ms. McGee, I'm not leaving."

"Not you, them," she said, pointing toward Bruce and Debbie. Part of her mind knew she was making things worse by talking about people no one, other than Ethel, could see.

Debbie walked in front of the detective and spoke directly to him. "Detective, it's Maggie's weapon. She did it. She killed our beloved superintendent, Mr. Carl Zimmerman." She pretended to pout and then she turned and looked at Maggie. "What are you going to do, Maggie, kill him, too? Go ahead, grab the knife and hack him, hack him to death. Do it now you witch, you murderous whore. Kill him."

CONNIE MYRES

Maggie stood there, her limbs moving as if she was having a seizure. She looked at the knife and then at the detective who was not taking his eyes off her. "No, I'm not going to kill. I'm not."

The two officers approached Maggie and handcuffed her and began reading the Miranda warning, "You have the right to remain silent. If you do say anything, it can be used against you in a court of law. You have the right to a lawyer present during any question. If you cannot afford a lawyer, one will be appointed for you if you so desire. Do you understand these rights?"

Maggie was preoccupied with Debbie and Bruce's laughter and taunting. She could not stop crying as she repeated, "Leave me alone; just leave me alone." She would have begun banging her head against the wall to

stop the thoughts, stop the visions, but an officer was gripping her handcuffed arm.

Detective Becker approached her. "Maggie, they are going to take you to the police station. There are people there who can help you."

"Why are you being so nice to her, Detective?" One officer asked as the other took Maggie out of the apartment. "She's the perp; it's plain as day."

Detective Becker ignored him. "Bag the evidence and search the apartment."

Maggie's brain had taken a leave of absence from its duty of rational thought. She was acting insane as she passed Ethel, not even acknowledging her words of *getting to the bottom of this*.

Ethel went to the apartment door. "Detective Becker, I need to speak with you."

"In the hallway, please." He watched as the officers took Maggie down the staircase and then looked at Ethel and the tears of black mascara streaming down her face. "I know this may sound crazy, but Maggie did not kill Mr. Zimmerman. It's this place, the spirits in this place. I know you don't believe me, but could you at least consider the possibility?"

As officers began investigating Maggie's apartment, he said. "I'll look at all the evidence, ma'am."

Ethel watched as officers strung more yellow barrier tape, blocking all the upper levels of the building. An officer helped Ethel to the elevator. When she reached the lobby, she looked through the window and saw a squad car drive away, with Maggie inside.

THIRTY-FIVE

A YOUNG WOMAN wearing a tight black skirt and holding a tablet in her hand, poked her head into Nora Bella's office. "Pendleton Books called while you were at lunch. They want a change in Dane Slegers contract," she cleared her throat, "they want us to take a smaller cut."

Nora Bella continued looking into the compact mirror and finished applying her red-wine lipstick. Then she checked her teeth, looking for pieces of parsley that may have lodged themselves in crevices, from the pasta she had at the deli. "Thanks, Yani."

She blew out a breath of frustration and began looking through her overflowing inbox of mail. She noticed Maggie's letter and picked it up, taking note that it was too thin for a manuscript. Its contents felt to be only a single sheet of paper.

"Maggie, is this your letter of resignation from the Raven's Ridge series?" she murmured to herself as she tossed it aside. "I can't deal with this right now. I'll read you later."

THIRTY-SIX

MAGGIE WORE A dark green inmate uniform as she sat behind bulletproof glass in the county jail visiting room. She saw a line of visitors, mostly women; come up the stairs, Ethel was one of them.

Ethel looked around the room until she noticed Maggie sitting and waiting. She sat in front of the glass and picked up the phone to the side of the window, Maggie did the same. "How are you doing in here, Maggie?"

Maggie shrugged. "They think I'm crazy."

"I know you're not crazy and I'll keep in communication with that Detective Becker. Even though he has to follow the rules, I sense that he knows there is something else happening. I'm on your side, Maggie, and I think the detective can help you."

Maggie looked down at the table. "I don't know how.

The knife was found in my apartment."

"It was *found* there; you weren't caught using it red handed." Ethel looked at Maggie's messy hair and drooping shoulders. She lowered her voice and said, "I'm working spells of protection for you, but the blackness

that's attached to you is powerful. Just do not give up. The more upset you are, the more you fuel it . . . And them. Stay positive."

Maggie's eyes were moist with tears. "Thank you, Ethel, you're a good friend. But I'm not having much luck staying positive, especially when I may be convicted of murder."

"You're innocent, Maggie, and the truth will come out."

"Even if the truth was to come out, Debbie and Bruce will do whatever they can to make me look guilty. It's hopeless."

Ethel changed the subject to something more pleasant, even though no matter what topic she chose, it would be depressing to a person trapped in a jail cell. A new recipe she was going to try, the flat tire she had repaired, and the sales at Lenny's Grocery would make a prisoner jealous.

The buzzer sounded.

"I guess my time's up." Ethel leaned toward the glass. "I'll be back for the next visitation day. And don't worry about your stuff, I've got it stored in my spare room. Is there anything you need me to do?"

Maggie shook her head. "Keep working on getting Debbie, Bruce, and Susie away from me . . . and that dark thing in the monk's robe." She paused, and then said, "Sometimes I see them here in the jail. They're making fun of me and saying things to the guards. Can people hear them? I mean, the guards and detectives, do you think their subconscious minds somehow hear the lies about me?"

"Depends," Ethel said, with a voice that scratched more than usual. "Most people have no ability to hear

them and no matter what Debbie and Bruce may say in their ears, it goes unheard and unacted upon. But sad to say, some weak individuals can hear, at least a little bit, and be influenced by the voices in their heads. Other people who hear them take it for what it is, spirit talk. They either ignore it or go into professions such as mine and use their sixth sense to communicate with spirits." Ethel forced a smile. "But don't you worry, I'll figure out a way to cast the evil spirits from your life."

She hung up and followed the rest of the visitors out of the room and down the stairs to the waiting area.

Maggie stayed seated. There was one more visitor to see. Minutes later the next group of people came through the door and into the room. Then she saw Jess walking toward her. Maggie wanted to call the guard over and refuse the visit, but she was curious to know why Jess was visiting and what she had to say.

Jess picked up the phone. "Hi, Maggie, how's it going?"

Maggie did not answer. How do you think it's going? She looked at Jess's happy face and jewel neckline blouse. The gold tassel necklace and matching bracelet looked expensive.

"Cat got you tongue?" Jess looked at the flat link chain bracelet and back to Maggie. "I know what you're thinking, *Is it real gold?* The answer is yes, it is. And I'm sorry to hear that my sunglasses, the ones you borrowed, were found in your superintendent's apartment. I had nothing to do with that. I don't know how they got there .

. . Unless you went off the deep end and killed the man while you were wearing them, and they fell off your pretty face while he fought you as you hacked him to

death. Too bad my name was engraved on them, and a witness saw you wearing them."

Maggie could not take the insults or Jess's need to flash her jewelry any longer. There was no way Jess made enough money working as a waitress at Flashers to afford anything but costume jewelry. Did she sell Cory's grandmother's jewelry? "Where'd you get the money for that?"

"Maggie, I'm really sorry things turned out this way. You're my best friend, always have been. Things got a little crazy this last year. I needed money and Cory needed . . . Well, you know what he needed. I'm sorry for all that. I hope you can forgive me."

CONNIE MYRES

Never, she thought. Then she saw Debbie and Bruce standing behind Jess. Had they been visiting her and talking to her, too? Was she one of the weak people that Ethel was talking about that could be influenced by their lies? Maybe it was not all Jess's fault, but she still did what she did by her own free will. "You didn't answer my question. Where'd you get the money to buy the jewelry?" "It's the funniest thing. Remember that lottery ticket you bought at Lenny's a while back? It must have fallen out of your purse when I drove you home after you got sloshed that night at your house. When I found it, I decided to scrape it off and see if it was a winner. You're not going to believe this, but it was; five-thousand-dollars

a week for life."

"That's my money, not yours." Maggie felt anger growing inside her. Ethel had warned her not to give the spirits and the dark entity negative energy to feed on, but she could not help it.

She saw the dark hooded entity standing in the far corner, next to a guard. Debbie and Bruce came up to the window, one on either side of Jess.

Debbie looked at Maggie. "You lose, Margaret. There is no way you can win against us. I once had an ampoule of your blood that I needed to finish the spell, but you kind of blew it all to pieces." Debbie looked toward the hooded figure and then back to Maggie. "I'm sure you see him, but Bruce and I still need to give a piece of you to it so that the spell can be completed, and Bruce and I can live in ecstasy forever."

Bruce put his hand on top of Jess's head like a crab bloodsucker and looked at Maggie. "Somehow you keep climbing out of the quicksand we lay in front of you, like a rat that can wiggle its way through the tiniest crevice. I have to hand it to you, Maggie, you are quite resilient. It's not so easy to destroy you, and believe me, we've tried."

"But not this time," Debbie said, touching Jess's shoulder, causing her to twitch. "Our friend, over there in the black robe, needs you to live in absolute anguish for the rest of your physical life so that he can feed off you. In exchange, it'll give us what we want . . . Deal?"

No frickin' deal.

Bruce and Debbie began talking in Jess's ears, each repeating vile and filthy words. *Kill yourself. Kill yourself. You're a whore and a thief. Go home now and drown your sorrows in alcohol and pills. Do it now.*

Jess began to wring her hands as if she could sense spirits were planting thoughts into her head. She looked at Maggie's horrified face. "What's wrong, Maggie?"

Maggie began to hyperventilate. "Jess, don't listen to the voices in your head. They're telling you lies. They're trying to get you to do . . . bad things."

"I've got to go." Jess stood abruptly, causing the plastic chair to tip over.

Maggie began screaming, a desperate attempt to save Jess. "They're following you. Don't listen to them. Don't do it, Jess. Don't do what they say." She began pounding on the glass, trying to break through as she continued to scream.

The guards approached Maggie and grabbed hold of her. "You're going to the hole."

Maggie lost it. She fought the guards and screamed all the way to a holding cell. Its large windows made it easy for guards to observe violent inmates. They tied her to *the chair* and closed the door. Frothy drool ran down her chin. The guards left, and she was alone in the room. Almost alone. The dark hooded entity was waiting for her. It approached her, enveloped her like a robed vampire, and began feeding on her. The more she fought the restraints and tried to escape, the darker the entity became. She felt her soul weakening and her mind breaking. She could think no more, she had to escape, but there was no escape. It was as if she was being raped and she had to separate her mind from her body to survive it. She was defeated.

The guards watched Maggie from the guardroom and on the monitors. They watched as her screaming subsided, replaced by her body twitching and her head moving side to side. "What's wrong with her? She's acting like she's having a seizure. We'd better get the nurse down here."

By the time the nurse arrived Maggie was limp, her head bent back with an open mouth, and her wide-open eyes stared at the ceiling. A guard escorted the nurse into Maggie's cell. With a gloved hand, he felt for a pulse on

the side of her neck, listened to her heart, and examined her pupils. "Ms. McGee, my name's Brent, I'm a nurse. Can you hear me?"

Maggie began mumbling nonsensical words, at least to everyone in the room. In a childlike voice, she rambled. "It's feeding on me. Where is the necklace? The teddy bear's neck is twisted. Where is Becker?"

"We need to get her to the emergency room and then when she's stable, transfer her to Port Glenn Psychiatric Hospital. Call an ambulance. I'll notify Doctor Aditya Suharto."

While the guard released Maggie from the restraints, the nurse looked around the room.

"What are you looking for, Brent?" The guard asked, watching his eyes dart about the cell.

"I don't know," he said, putting the stethoscope back around his neck. "A chill suddenly came over me. I guess it was nothing." He looked at Maggie. "Did she say the name, Becker?"

"Yeah, I think it was Becker. I wonder if she was thinking about Detective Becker, he's the one following her case."

The paramedics arrived and took Maggie away. Her conscious mind was locked in a rusty steel box in the back of her cranium, not to be opened until it was safe to come out. Maggie had lost the battle.

THE END

Thank you for reading!

ConnieMyres.com

Recommended Book

Unrestrained
A Paranormal Psychological Thriller
(Rancor, #2)

Now committed to a psychiatric hospital, Maggie McGee's only hope for help comes from Ethel, a seer. But will Ethel believe the psychiatrist's diagnosis? Will she be able to stop the evil spirits? Or will she become a victim herself?

Visit ConnieMyres.com

or

Books2Read.com/ConnieMyres

Also by Connie

STANDALONE BOOKS

Twisted Intentions, Beneath the White Veil, Ring, Haunting of Ender House, Rest Stop Terror, Solus, Who Killed Sweet Violet?, Lucifer's Island, Raven's Ridge

PACIE ROSE MYSTERIES

Pacie Rose Mysteries (Books 1–3)
Slenderman, Hornet, Wolf
Jezebel, My Name is Mr. Dibble

RANCOR

Rancor: A Paranormal Psychological Thriller (Books 1 & 2)
Sinister Attachments, Unrestrained

SEVEN SEALS REDUX

Seven Seals Redux: The Complete Apocalyptic Novel Series (Books 1–7)
White Horse, Red Horse, Black Horse, Pale Horse, Tribulation, Signs, Trumpets

SUSPENSE STORIES

Suspense Stories #1: Raven's Ridge, Lucifer's Island, Sinister Attachments

WATCH FOR SPOOKY SHORTS

Spooky Shorts A-G: A Collection of Creepy Short Stories
Apple Pie, Black-Eyed Kids, Creature, Dungeon, Electric, Fairy, Genie, House, Ice, Joker, Kiss, Lucid, Minion, Neighbor, Obelisk, Pattern, Quest, Rumor, Squatch, Time, Underwold, Visitor, Wolf, X-axis, Yellow, ZoZo

The complete list of books can be found at
ConnieMyres.com
or
Visit my Books2Read Author Page

CONNIE MYRES, a multi-genre author specializing in horror, mystery, suspense, and science fiction, has been spinning thrilling tales since her childhood in Michigan. From a young age, she captivated her audiences—children she babysat—by weaving them into her suspense-filled narratives, igniting an insatiable love for storytelling.

Inspired by the works of literary masters such as Dean Koontz and Stephen King, Connie has crafted her own unique style that keeps readers on the edge of their seats. Her vivid, dynamic stories, filled with intrigue and surprise, mirror her own multi-faceted life. Not only a talented writer, Connie is a registered nurse and a developer, showing her knack for both caring for others and creating immersive digital worlds.

In the future, Connie plans to join the digital nomad movement, allowing her love for adventure and new experiences to fuel her compelling narratives further. For now, she continues to captivate and inspire from her home base in Michigan, crafting stories that both engage and terrify her readers.

Stay connected with Connie through her website at ConnieMyres.com, where you can explore her wide range of books and short stories, and join her on this incredible storytelling journey.

FEATHER AND FERMION PUBLISHING

Feather and Fermion Publishing is a Michigan-based publisher that was founded in 2014. Our mission is to provide readers with thrilling and entertaining stories across a variety of genres, including horror, mystery, suspense, thriller, science fiction, and fantasy. We publish original fiction under our two imprints: Oort Cloud Books and White-Knuckle Books.

Author Connie Myres owns Feather and Fermion Publishing.

VISIT CONNIE'S WEBSITE

Visit Connie's website and find her books, blog, sales, and more.

ConnieMyres.com

CONNIE MYRES

AUTHOR

.